Let Me Tell You a Story:
Small Stories from a Large Family

LACHLAN MACKINNON

DEDICATION

To Elizabeth Buchanan,
one of the finest people I've ever known who always told me,
writing is cheaper than therapy.
I love you, Gram.

ACKNOWLEDGEMENTS

Special thanks to Meg Salkin and Megan MacKinnon
for support and encouragement.

Double secret, triple dog, extra special thanks to Dad, Warburton, Bel,
Morrighan, Feowyn, Malcolm, Ian, Barbara, Declan
and any other family or friends
who graciously gave me permission to write about
and make fun of our past.

Thank you to Charles Abou-Chebl, Phil Goldberg, John Kalman,
and Arjay Protacio for helping bring this to life.

Thank you Errybody for reading.

To: _____

I am not a writer.

It is important you know before we go any further. Most of these stories were just quick little things I would post on Facebook to try to get one of my friends to laugh. (Don't send me a friend request. I don't know you.) I would write a story if I saw someone was having a bad day or if someone said something reminded me of a story. I'm an OK storyteller. If we were at a party together, I could probably make you laugh. But, the chances of me being at a party are slim anyway. I don't really like parties. Or people.

I argued with friends who told me I should publish a book of these stories for a long time. I figured unless you knew my family and me then you wouldn't really get what was funny about a lot of these things. This whole book is essentially one giant run on sentence! The other thing I want to tell you before we get too far is I wrote this entire book while I was on the clock at my job.

This is also important to know for my Father. Oh, I'm sure he will be proud of me for having written a book, but if he knew I wrote it WHILE I was being paid for doing something else would just make him so much happier. He believes pilferage from an employer is one of the only ways left in America for the little guy to get one over on the Man. It can be in the form of light bulbs, toilet paper, or time. If it was stolen from your job, then it was worth its weight in gold. He wouldn't even consider it stealing. It's pilfering. All my life I was lead to believe this argument would stand up in a court of law. I'm not sure it will, I'm not a lawyer. The proudest achievement of my father's 40 year career of working for the railroad all the live long day was when he tore his Achilles' tendon while he was shaking a vending machine in the companies cafeteria because it just stole a quarter from him and he was able to make a worker's compensation claim against the railroad for his injuries because it happened while he was on the clock.

His union made sure they paid for his surgery and he still received a paycheck for the 6 to 8 weeks he sat on his ass watching John Wayne movies and smoking pot all summer! It was a different time back then. I don't have a union and you can't buy anything from the vending machines at my job for less than 2 dollars so the least I can do is take 45 minutes in the morning to write some silly story will get over 40 "LIKES" on social media. I am glad you are along for this ride. Put this book in your bathroom and read one story at a time or take an hour and read the whole thing, I don't know your life! I hope you get a chuckle out of it.

Thanks.

Cast of Characters

My dad- **Bill MacKinnon born 1945**

In a lot of ways my dad is the star of the show. He's quite possibly the smartest person I've ever met. He's read every book. He's seen every movie and heard every record. If you laugh at any of the stories in this book, there is a high probability you're laughing at something my dad did. He doesn't realize certain things he does or says are ridiculous and that's what makes it funny. If you and I were out somewhere and I did something made you laugh, I probably did it TO make you laugh. My dad does things the way he wants and is not interested in how it looks or sounds. The very first time he met my wife while we were dating we went to an Irish festival in Berea. As soon as we parked his truck we walked toward the entrance while my dad was taking a leak in the parking lot. He wasn't being impolite, he just really had to pee...

There is an ongoing family debate as to whether or not my dad is attracted to crazy women or (more likely) he drives women crazy after they marry him. He's been married 5 times we know of, it is altogether possible there's a sixth wife in there who I never met but she lived in Canada, so I'm not sure it even counts. I can tell you now his current wife Kay is probably the best of the bunch and if I know her the way I think I do, she will murder him before he has a chance to meet wife number 6. Or 7 depending on the exchange rate. When

I get the phone call saying she's murdered my dad, I will be sad but at the same time I will want to know what he did to deserve it...l wonder if the stories about him in this book can be used as evidence? Anyway, you should also know his real name is Warburton, as was his father's. My dad was the 7th generation first born to be named Warburton but he hated the name so much at the age of 13, he decided his name was Bill. He still named HIS first-born son Warburton. My dad and Kay are both currently retired and probably arguing about something at their home in Smithville West Virginia. Don't worry Dad is deaf, so he can't hear what Kay is saying.

My mother- **Laure MacKinnon 1954-1999**

So if the funny stories involve my dad, the not-so-funny stories involve my mom. This is not entirely fair, for most of my life my mom was a great mother. Funny, smart, attentive, and nurturing. After my parents divorced, things started to go downhill for her. By the time I was in High School, she was a full-blown alcoholic. Doctors will tell you she died from cancer, but people who were around then will tell you she drank herself to death. Many of my own personal issues with depression, insomnia and insecurity were probably inherited from her. We had a terrible relationship from the time I was a teenager until her death, much of it was my fault. When she was angry with me, she would say I was just like my dad. I suspect one of the reasons she and I had such a tumultuous relationship was because we were so similar. To her credit, I didn't even realize both my sister Bel and my brother Warburton were my stepbrother and stepsister until I was 12 years old and even though it may be true, we never acknowledged it. They're just my brother and sister and that is because of her. She raised them right there with the rest of us with no favoritism shown to her own children. I also have to credit her with making me straight edge. My way of rebelling against my parents was to do everything the opposite of the way they did when I was a teenager. Although common amongst angry teenagers, by the time most people reach their mid-twenties they become resigned to be their parents. Watching the way she drank made such a profound effect on me, I stopped drinking when I was 16 or 17. Well with the exception of getting shitfaced on a dare when I was 27, I never drink, smoke or do drugs. Like Nancy Reagan, I just say no.

Warburton MacKinnon- Born 1971

Birth order is important in large families and being the first-born son brought with it certain pressures from my dad. Not only was he saddled with the name but Warburton was expected to be the work-out buddy and shining example of what my dad expected out of us when I was young. My dad was never the kind of guy to put giant expectations on any of us kids. He didn't force us into anything, but he also did not like for us to disagree with him. 99% of the time Warburton would go along with whatever my dad said. Maybe this was because they are incredibly similar or maybe Warburton didn't want to disappoint the old man, I don't know?

Warburton enlisted in the Marines at 17 and got as far away from our family as he could. I can't say I blame him, but it created a distance between he and I that still exists to this day. He was discharged after his service in the Gulf war and settled and eventually married in Milwaukee. He's the only child of my father's second wife and he grew up never knowing his mother. As terrible as my relationship with my mother was at least I knew her, even when I was young I wondered how he felt about missing out on that relationship. I would have asked him but he was too busy beating the crap out of me at the time.

Belphoebe MacKinnon- Born 1974

Bel was the only child my father had with wife number 3. She's been a model big sister in almost every way. When we were younger and unsure of something Bel was the one we would go to. When my mother started to really lose her way, Bel stepped up and took charge. Bel raised my younger sister Feowyn and since she is the most successful of all the siblings, a strong case could be made Belphoebe was the best parent any of us ever had. She taught me how to tie a necktie before my freshman year and helped me forge my mother's signature on papers that came home from school. She's always been there for us, the more you needed- the more she gave.

But before you think I am canonizing her, let me tell
you with the possible exception of my wife, she is the
biggest bitch I've ever known! Bel and I were very
close growing up, but the last 2 or 3 years we lived
together at home we did not speak! At all. We were
very different people in high school, she was popular
and got invited to all the parties. Her and her large
circle of friends remained close all through high school
and college and eventually all the girls paired off with
the guys and got married. They are all still friends to
this day! That's insane to me. I was extremely
unpopular in high school, never got invited to any
parties, and to this day only have about 3 solid friends. I
was recently in a grocery store when a kid I went to
high school with came up and started talking to me. I
looked him right in the eye, denied my name was
Lachlan MacKinnon and hurried into another aisle. I
am an asshole. Bel is not. High school happened to
coincide with when my mom was at her worst, so it was
rough for all of us. Bel made sure everyone had enough
to eat while I was up in my room playing guitar and
being Emo. We didn't see eye to eye. Through it all, we
were on the same team and I'd like to think we helped
each other make it livable for the younger kids.

Belphoebe busted her ass working multiple jobs to put
herself through college with. She became a teacher, got
married, and has 4 girls of her own. I see things in each
of my nieces are the spitting image of their mother and
it makes me happy to no end. Like two soldiers who
survived the hairiest of battles, we never talk about how
we were to each other in high school and we use the

word 'Grovewood" to imply when things were shitty. It took some time but Bel recently started talking to me again.

Lachlan MacKinnon - Born 1976

The word genius is thrown about way to easily these days...

Morrighan MacKinnon- Born 1977

Morrighan has the middle child syndrome and it's probably my fault. I was a horrible big brother to her. When we were both in grade school she would get the same teacher, I had the year before and those teachers probably gave her a way harder time then they should've. Teachers started drinking heavily after dealing with my shenanigans every day for a year. The last thing they wanted to see show up in their classrooms the next year was another MacKinnon. I tried to help her out though. The teachers I had from 5th grade until 8th grade all quit and went to teach at another school immediately after having me as a student, except my fifth-grade teacher Sister Marie Caniece. She took the honorable way out and died. Morrighan was a model student with good grades, no attitude problems etc., It's probably a little late for apologies, but I'm sorry. It's not easy to follow a showstopper like me! When we were really young no matter what we were playing Mo would whip out her secret weapon - The Magic Finger! If we were playing

tag and you were about to tag her she would stop, point
her index finger at you and go
"DOOOOOOOOOOOOOOO". To this day I am not
quite sure what the magic finger was supposed to do?
Freeze us? Kill us? I guess you'll have to wait for her
book to find out, all I know is it would make us angry
so when we did tag her, it was with a little extra
emphasis. She'd usually start crying and run to Mom.
She spent most of our childhood crying and running to
our mom.

Just like Bel, she worked two jobs to put herself
through college and she is now some kind of supervisor
at an insurance company. I actually get mad at her
every time I see one of their horrible commercials.

Feowyn MacKinnon- Born 1982

Where to start with her??? Feowyn has had an uphill
battle since day one. Immediately after she was born,
my dad went away to prison for a two-year stretch and
when he came back things were never really the same
with him and my mom. And on top of the double
whammy of being born on Christmas that is kind of a
rip-off, being saddled with a totally unpronounceable
name. The story I heard was my mom liked the name
Fiona and my dad liked the name Branwynn so they got
high AF and decided to combine the name into Feowyn
(pronounced - REE-DICK- ULUSSS) on the bright
side, at least it isn't Warburton! Of all my siblings Fe
and I probably have the most similar personalities. I've

better taste in music and am just a little funnier. She is a better writer and far more successful. We both get insomnia and depression but she missed out on the crippling insecurity. She's had things harder than I ever did. Yet, she's been the most self-confident person I know. In our entire lives, I've only ever been really mad at her one time. It was because she broke the needle on my turntable! Sorry for punching you Fe, but needles were like 40 bucks!

When I was 15, her and I hopped in my sister's car and went to the drive thru at McDonald's. The car we were driving had sub-par brakes and I didn't have a license, as we were slowly pulling around to pay for our food I hit the car in front of us. I got out and used my Southern charm and boyish good looks to convince the old women I hit there was no damage and it was an honest mistake. Thankfully she agreed and declined to call the cops. We got our food and went home. I tell you this story now because like a trusted cellmate she kept this incident a secret for 25 years. You can't ask for much more out of a kid sister. Feowyn and I've matching Black Power tattoos, hers says Soul Sister mine says Soul Brother. There is no one else in the world who would think it was a good idea for two fair skinned Irish siblings to get this particular tattoo but she thought it was a great idea!

Feowyn is an over-achiever in every way, she put herself through college and grad school and is now the principal at the highest ranking High School in the

Cleveland School District and the only one of my siblings who loaned me money over the years.

Malcolm MacKinnon- Born 1986

This Fucker... By the time he was born, my parents' marriage was all but over. What Bel was for Feowyn, I tried to be for Malcolm but even I know Bel did as much for him as I did. My job with the two younger kids was really to make them laugh and try to take their minds off of things when they were bad. Bel did the more concrete parenting jobs like making sure homework was done and they bathed regularly. Malcolm was my dude from the start and I turned down many invites to go out with friends, so I could stay home and party with him. Not because I had to or felt obligated, I just loved hanging out with him. I still hold some guilt when I was 19 and started dating Megan I chose to hang out with her as often as I could and I feel like I left him in the lurch. When he probably needed me the most I wasn't there for him. I don't know if he sees it this way, but I do. When things got out of control with my mom, Malcolm went to live with my dad in Atlanta for high school, after he graduated he moved back to Cleveland and my dad retired and settled in West Virginia. Nothing much phases Malcolm, Dude is bulletproof. Literally! He got shot in his neck one night, got in his car and drove himself to the hospital. He's never given me a whole lot of details about what actually happened night, the closest I ever got to an explanation was him admitting he was hanging with the wrong people...

When Malcolm was a baby, Bel and I were setting up the Christmas tree and putting the lights up for the holidays. Malcolm crawled over to the tree, reached up and grabbed a shiny red, glass ornament and before you could say "Hey, where are our parents?" He took a giant bite out of it. The sound of glass shattering all over a baby's face is truly an aural delight! We ran over to him expecting the worst and this hardened infant just spit out whatever glass he didn't swallow and crawled away! I would have been in intensive care on life support, but Malcolm walked away without a scratch on him! That's pretty much how he is today, although he probably drinks a little too much. And I definitely disagree with his politics but other than that, he just motors along like the machine he is. He works for the same insurance company Morrighan works for even though he doesn't believe in the idea of insurance at all.

Megan MacKinnon - Born - None of your business

I met Megan my junior year in high school (1992-93). I had been politely asked not to return to Villa Angela-St. Joseph's and I was going to be stuck going to Collinwood. I was pretty nervous about going there because all I ever heard were terrible things about the school. In my mind I pictured East High from the movie Lean on Me. Which wasn't far off, except there were more white kids in the movie school. My best friend Joe Holzheimer worked at Sandy's the neighborhood ice cream spot and one of his co-workers was Megan Mullally, who was the other white kid stuck going to Collinwood. He introduced us before the school year, so both of us could at least have one ally. Megan was immediately attracted to my movie star good looks and winning personality (Can you blame her?) so we made a habit of cutting school and going to do more important things like watch movies or make out on her mom's new couch.

Sometime before the end of our junior year we broke up. It was your typical teenage heartbreak story and it was very hard for Megan to watch me out on the town banging every hot chick I could. As you'll learn in this book 17-year-old Lachlan was pretty fuckin great! The women wanted to be with me and the Men wanted to be me! I was voted the *Sassiest Boy in America* by Sassy magazine like 3 years in a row! After about three years of her constant begging and pleading to give her a second chance, I had a hole in my social calendar so I decided to throw her a bone. That was 22 years ago and we have been together ever since!

She is the best wife a guy could ask for, she made sure the bills were paid the entire time my band was off breaking attendance records on tour. She has nursed me back to health anytime I've been sick and she blessed me with the coolest son of all time. She shows up in a lot of these stories and believe me when I tell you she's not happy about it. She is not a big fan of me making light of embarrassing situations but let's me do it anyway. She is the best and I really hope she doesn't hurt herself rolling her eyes at these stories.

But if she does, God forbid then ladies, give me a call!

Bologna Summer 1985:
A time that will live in infamy

So at some point during the Reagan years my father (and everyone else) got laid off from Conrail. There was a plethora of Collinwood dads home during the days. My mother had gone back to work and my dad was doing Mr. Mom duties for the summer.

Dad was going grocery shopping and he asked me to watch my younger sister...and then I made the mistake that would haunt my summer. "Hey Dad, can you buy some bologna for lunches??" I asked.

"Baloney? You like garbage???"

I assured him, yes! I did in fact like bologna. Because I was 9 and I guess I didn't know any better. Dad came home an hour later and put food away in the refrigerator he handed me a giant, heavy white deli package. "What is this?" I asked. Without looking up from the fridge Dad said, "That's the friggin bologna you asked for!"

Now, I was no expert but I had been to a grocery store before and I had seen bologna before. It usually came in yellow and red plastic containers and had at most 12 slices in them. You had to eat it pretty fast because those last 2 slices were pretty gnarly after about a week! So, as I opened up this package I was hit with the stank of something clearly not sanctioned by Mr. Oscar Meyer. No, the bargain shopper my dad was bought me 5lbs of fresh garlic bologna from Sam the butcher. There was nothing in the world quite as scary as my father losing money, so I was gonna have to make it work with this bootleg bologna whether I liked it or not. There was no amount of mustard you could put on this shit to try to fool your mouth you were eating normal, eckrich bologna. One lunch and already I knew I was in trouble.

After about 3 days of trying to choke this stuff down I finally broke down and told my dad I think he bought the wrong kind of lunch meat and I didn't really like this garlic bullshit. Dad was really cool about it. He looked me in the eye and said, "I don't give a good goddamn if you like it or not, you're gonna eat every last piece!" Clearly, honesty was not an option.

During lunches from that point on, I would enjoy my mustard bread as I calmly slipped the bologna into my pocket without my sisters noticing, which wasn't too hard because they were busy eating delicious mouth-watering peanut butter and jelly sandwiches like normal human beings while I stuffed my pockets full of greasy garlic bologna, excused myself to the bathroom, and flushed it down the toilet.

This was not the best solution for several reasons. First, we had one bathroom for 7 or 8 people and you did NOT want to be responsible for clogging the can. Secondly, my mom asked me what I was doing to my pants because they all smelled like garlic!

They were on to me so I had to go to plan B.

Plan B involved me eating the bread and mustard, but taking the bologna and when no one was looking, throwing it behind the pantry shelf in the kitchen. Plan B worked like a charm for the next two or three weeks until thank the Jesus we were out of bologna!!! I was never so thankful to pull an empty Ziploc from the fridge! Lunch with my sisters soon went back to being a pretty fun part of the day! Peanut butter, jelly, tuna fish, soup, grilled cheese anything, but disgusting garlic bologna!!!

Life was good.

My dad would ask us if we smelled anything weird in the kitchen and we acted like we had no idea what he was talking about because we rarely did. But as the summer went on and the temperature rose, we started to smell it too. It was a very faint, almost garlicky aroma of something rotten. I had totally forgotten about the 5 lbs. of meat I had thrown behind our cereal cupboard that landed directly on a windowsill and baked in direct sunlight all summer.

My dad went insane with the smell in the kitchen. He was like Gene Hackman in The Conversation, all day long he took things out of the cupboards, cleaned every shelf until one day the unthinkable happened...

I was at my friend Brian's house when I heard my dad scream my name from down the street. There weren't a lot of kids named Lachlan in north Collinwood back then, so I knew it was me. As I ran down the street, my sister Bel peddled her bike as fast as she could in the opposite direction. I could tell by the look in her eyes this was bad...

I walked into my house and directly into my dad's fist. He dragged me into the kitchen to show me what he found when he moved the pantry. Sitting on a paper plate at my spot was my dinner that night, 5 lbs. of rotten sundried, brown garlic bologna.

"Would you like mustard with your dinner, Mr. MacKinnon?" my dad said with an evil smile.

He made me sit in my chair and told me I couldn't get up until I ate all of it.

I cried and wished for Death's sweet relief until 9 pm. I sat there and listened to Dad scrub the floor, wall, and put the pantry back. I listened to him about all the starving kids who wished they had bologna to eat and how lucky I was. To be honest, I missed most of what he said because my sisters laughed at me through the back window. Between that and the smell of this pile of rancid deli in front of me, I may have passed out at some point. Finally, Dad grabbed the plate in front of me, threw it in the garbage, and told me to go to bed. Even now 30 years later, if I close my eyes, I can still smell nasty garlic bologna. Brutal.

Collinwood's Wide World of Sports

I've never taken an IQ test. Most of my day is telling hillbilly truck drivers what dock to back in to and a monkey could do. The other day I told my son a story and he said I was pretty smart. As soon as he said that, I thought about the story I am about to tell you. Not only is it the stupidest thing I'd ever done but it very well may be the stupidest thing ANYONE has ever done! And including the time my beautiful wife swam in the ocean while she was on her period!

One of my favorite shows to watch on weekends when I was a kid was ABC's Wide World of Sports. Sometimes you'd get lucky and catch a Marvin Hagler fight or an old episode of battle of the network stars with some Marilu Henner sideboob action, but more often than not, it would be something boring like a bicycle race. This was before cable reached the east side, so one took what one could get.

The early 80's were obsessed with bicycle culture. Kevin Bacon and Kevin Costner both had movies about pensive, emo bicycle messengers or some shit. There was *Breaking Away* with Dennis Quaid and the BMX movie *Rad*. Queen had multiple hit songs about riding bikes and every girl at St. Jerome's wore spandex shorts under their skirts. I sat on my couch and watched Greg Lemond win some fruity European bike race. I thought it was pretty cool when they broke tape crossing the finish line. Racing friends became a common practice among Collinwood's bicycle enthusiasts and since my BMX had no brakes what so ever, I discovered I won my fair share of those races. I also went through more than a few pairs of shoes while dragging my feet along the pavement trying to stop my bike, but that was a separate issue.

One early Sunday morning, while the good Catholic kids were at church I putzed around town on my bike drank a Big Gulp and looked for something to do. I rode up to Grovewood pool to see if I could get into a basketball game, but there was no one around. I rode across the street to see if anyone was playing at Humphrey's field with no luck. I sat on the bleachers and took a break. As I sat there, finished a 64-ounce breakfast Coke, I thought about the cool bike race I watched the day before and I said to myself, "I bet if I pedaled fast enough, I could break right through a tennis court net."

Now, when a 12-year-old kid has a totally bitchin idea like this very little time is spent thinking about safety or logistics. In fact, most common sense was thrown out the window as I started thinking about how much sweet adolescent booty I was gonna get. Once everyone found out what I did! I psyched myself up until I was at the far end of the tennis court and planned my approach.

All of a sudden, I was Doc Brown from *Back to the Future*. I figured if I got my bike up to 88 miles an hour, the tennis net would snap in two and the crowd would go wild!

I took a deep breath and pedaled towards glory. I rode as hard and as fast as I could right towards the middle of the net. I motored like Sister Christian all jacked up on Jolt cola. I closed my eyes and leaned forward as I came up to the net and...bang! I was clotheslined by two-inch steel line that supported the net. I flew backward, my bike sailed forward and into the fence. I hit the concrete on the tennis courts with the full weight of my body and ambitions. The back of my head crashed into the ground with a sickening thud. I've never hit a cantaloupe with a baseball bat, but I am pretty sure that's what it sounded like!

I opened my eyes and tried to catch my breath, but it was hard to breathe through a crushed windpipe. I may have lost consciousness at some point. I s lowly stood up and looked around to make sure no one had witnessed what I did. Thank God this was an era before cell phone cameras. Humphrey's Field was still empty, as I staggered towards my bike I leaned over and violently puked up my breakfast. My vomit was carbonated and it burned my throat coming back up. The back of my head was bleeding and my neck felt like it had been stepped on by the Cleveland Browns defense. I tried to gather myself the best I could to ride my bike home. There was a loud ringing in my ears as I struggled to stay on my bike. I ran into my house and for once no one was in the bathroom. I put a cold rag against the back of my head. There was already a large purple bruise forming on my throat. I took my t-shirt off and saw large scrapes on the back of both shoulders and a Rorschach test blood stain on the back of my shirt. My sister Feowyn was in the kitchen and saw me struggling to drink a glass of water. She asked what happened and I didn't have the heart to tell my 6-year old kid sister my Adams apple had been crushed doing an Evil Knievel impression. I meekly told her I had an accident on my bike. She put some ice cubes in a towel for me and I proceeded to do the one thing someone with a fresh head injury should never do--I took a nice long nap.

When I woke up I had a headache that would last me three days, but the ringing in my ears was gone so I figured I was ok. I was probably nursing a serious concussion but I was way too embarrassed to tell my mom. If I would've gone to the doctor then CTE would have been discovered 15 years earlier and Will Smith would have starred in a movie about me and my massive head wound. The next day at school I was sporting a giant knot on the back of my head and a crazy looking bruise across my neck but thankfully most of my classmates already figured I was being abused at home so no one really asked about my new look.

The Strip Steak

When my father worked in Pittsburgh he bought a house in Weirton, West Virginia. Weirton is a small town just over the Pennsylvania border. It was another in a long line of dead. Industrial towns, famous for producing steel and punk rock photographers. (Hi, Jay Brown!)

My dad loved it there. It wasn't a big city, but it wasn't the middle of nowhere either. They had a KFC and a grocery store, but that was about it.

When I was about 18 or 19, I went to visit him for a few days. We woke up pretty early one morning and went kayaking. After putting around in the river for a couple hours, we decided to head back to town. My dad asked, "Hey, are you hungry?" Like he had never met me. (For future reference, the answer to that question is always going to be YES. I may be dead on the inside, but I am always hungry!!)

"There is a bar by the house that has great strip steaks for 4.99 during lunch hours, I think we can still hit."

"Sounds great. Can we stop at home and shower first? I'm still all sweaty from kayaking."

Dad laughed, "This is West Virginia. No one cares."

We pulled into the parking lot and there was a sign in the window advertising the $4.99 businessman lunch from 11am-5pm. It was only about 3 pm, so we had plenty of time. It was a pretty hot morning and my t – shirt was damp with sweat. Clearly, it wasn't a four-star restaurant or anything, but I still felt gross. I looked at my dad, he wore cut -off jean shorts cut way too short. The lining of the pockets stuck out. He wore black work boots with no socks and a long-sleeved flannel shirt. Compared to him I looked like I was going to a job interview.

I was starving. We walked in and as if I wasn't feeling weird enough, I realized we were gonna eat lunch at a strip club in Weirton, West Virginia! "Dad, you didn't tell me it was a freaking strip club!!" I shouted.

"What? Oh relax, they have great steaks!" He responded.

It wasn't the first time I had been to a strip club, hell this wasn't even the first time I had been to a strip club with my dad! But there is never going to be a time when I am comfortable with it. I am 40 and I recently watched a movie had a sex scene in it with him. I'm pretty sure this movie was rated pg-13, but I was still uncomfortable because he was sitting in the same room as I was! The other thing that bothered me is my dad is not a strip club kind of guy. I mean, he is a dude, so naturally he is a pervert. But he's not the kind of pervert who hangs out at naked lady bars. He *is* the kind of pervert who enjoys a 5 dollar steak though!

The place was mostly empty as we sat down and ordered our lunch. The bar was shaped like a T with a long runway in the middle where the girls would dance. We sat at the first two seats near the top of the T in a place where if I was a woman taking off my clothes I would say to myself, *those two sweaty guys are probably just here for lunch.* But, I guess I don't think like a stripper because about one minute after placing an order, there was a naked woman dancing in front of us.

Is this story weirding you out yet?

As soon as this woman came over to us she said, "Hi Bill, I finished that book you gave me!"

If you are uncomfortable going to a strip club with your dad, you will be markedly more uncomfortable when you find out not only is your father on a first name basis with a West Virginia stripper, but apparently, they are in a fucking book club together!!!!

This young woman was beautiful (well, Weirton
beautiful. She was probably a 6 in Cleveland) and naked.
I was sweaty and uncomfortable. My dad didn't think
anything of it, I tried to hide a boner and lost my appetite
while the old fucker is having a serious discussion of
postmodern feminist literature!!! The man is an enigma.

When our food came out, they finished up their
dissertation and she went over to dance for some other old
coot. All in all, it was one of the more surreal lunches I
have ever had, but I gotta say it was a really good five-
dollar steak!!

Fuck Michigan

I went to Villa Angela- St. Joseph's for my first two years of high school. It was also the first two years the schools merged and all the older teachers were still learning how to deal with the opposite sex. One way they dealt with this was all the St. Joe's teachers thought all the girls were innocent and never caused any trouble. This was not so.

My friends and I were talking about this when a girl named Taneesha came up to us. I still followed sports pretty heavy in my sophomore year. I had a discussion about how Desmond Howard did not deserve to win the Heisman trophy year. He was a really great kick/punt returner who was ok as a receiver, but not the best college player in the country. That year Ty Detmer had set all kinds of passing records at BYU and *he* deserved the award.

I had never spoken to Taneesha before, in fact I kind of thought she was mute because I never even heard her speak. Taneesha came up to our group and said, "Desmond Howard is my cousin!" Both Desmond Howard and Elvis Grbac were great football players at St. Joes four years earlier and caused a minor northeast Ohio scandal when they both chose to go to the University of Michigan (gross) instead of Ohio State. It made both players pretty disliked among my group of friends at the school. That part didn't bother me, as I generally hated everyone. Especially in 1991.

So, I responded to Taneesha's statement by saying, "Well, I'm sure he is a great guy, but he still is not a Heisman trophy winner!" My friends laughed. Taneesha pulled back and punched me in the face!!!

If a girl punches a guy, for the guy it's a lose-lose situation. If he punches her back, he is a scumbag because what kind of an animal punches a woman???? And if he doesn't do anything he is a giant pussy who just got jacked by a girl!!! I was a giant pussy who just got punched in the face by a mute girl.

Our teacher sent us both down to the principal's office where I sat in my normal chair and explained I didn't even know Taneesha or do anything that deserved to get rocked in the mouth. I was honestly kind of shocked at the whole thing. Taneesha apologized to me and whipped up some quick tears and babbled about "stress at home" or some shit AND THEY LET HER GO BACK TO CLASS!!!!

Father Tedesco and Sister Mary Owen spent the rest of the day trying to decide what to do with me. Their argument was they never had any issues with Taneesha but had several issues with me. They felt like two weeks of detention was an appropriate punishment for getting punched in the face. By a girl. I didn't complain. What was two more weeks of detention? That was where I did my homework before going to my job anyway.

This whole episode was brought up to my mother in another meeting at the end of year to justify the school asking me not to return for 11th grade. School administration felt my 1.3 GPA and overdue tuition payments coupled with driving mute girls to the point of assault was not the image they were trying to cultivate in their students.

For the record, not only did Desmond Howard NOT deserve the Heisman, but he also did not deserve the Super Bowl MVP in 1996. Fuck that dude. I hope Taneesha is doing well.

Couvade Syndrome

All I ever wanted to be in life is a good dad and husband. I was doing pretty well on the husband part when I found a hot girl who was willing to have sex with me and who made a hell of a sandwich. So, I locked that up at 22. After six or seven years of marriage, I finally wore Megan down on the kid's front. She realized that I was never gonna be the kind of guy with money in the bank or a great job, so she took solace in the fact that at least I had a steady job with good insurance. I wasn't a heroin addict and decided it was as good of a time as any.

It took us a long time to get pregnant, almost 4 years. I tried to make sure we didn't get stressed out. *If it happens, it happens* was my attitude. I'm not sure I believed in God, but I told myself if we couldn't get pregnant, then it was God's will and I would just become a better uncle. I wasn't about to spend money on fertility drugs or treatments. If Mother Nature said this planet could no longer afford to support any new MacKinnons, then who was I to argue? Eventually, Megan did get pregnant and we were so excited. We were also scared, nervous, anxious, and worried, but mostly excited. Especially after finding out that our "first child was going to be a masculine child," in the words of Luca Brasi.

The day we found out we were having a little boy was one of the happiest days of my life!

During my wife's pregnancy, everyone offered her advice and gave her dog-eared copies of books by Doctor Spock (not the Star Trek guy) and What to Expect When Expecting. No one really tells the husband anything, certainly nothing helpful! Oh sure, you'll get plenty of people tell you, "Save up for diapers" or "Take a lot of naps now." But no one ever told me about Couvade Syndrome, or that even if one were as unsympathetic as I was, that one would still suffer from sympathy pains.

Couvade Syndrome is defined by Webster's as "a practice among some primitive peoples in which a man, immediately preceding the birth of his child, ritualistically imitates the pregnancy and delivery of the mother." Frankly, I don't agree with this definition because in my experience I was not imitating anything! My body went through things I was unprepared for even 11 years later, I have still not recovered from. Because of this country's obvious matriarchy, we husbands just suffer in silence. No one talks about what men go through! Women get all the glory, but our pregnancy was much harder on me than it was on Megan. And no one held my hand! In an effort to help my brothers in the world, I am writing this to let you know about my experience with Couvade Syndrome. If I can manage to warn just one expectant father out there, then this will have been worth it.

Weight Gain: The first and most noticeable symptom.

During the nine months of my wife's pregnancy, she only gained 14 pounds. She was very conscious about what she ate and was careful not to overindulge. I, on the other hand, gained 30 pounds, mostly due to stress eating double cheeseburgers on my way home from work. Women may give you the "I'm eating for two" bullshit, but they aren't. They have a human being growing inside them, taking up all the room in their midsection. Their stomachs can only hold a tiny amount of food anyway! Plus, that baby is constantly kicking them in the kidneys, so a pregnant woman pees 36 times a day. It's almost like she is on a diet! Meanwhile, the father just washed down 7 doughnuts with a vanilla milkshake at 8 am, and he can only pee when you are in REM sleep. And this is all before the baby is born; once he comes along and starts breastfeeding, that baby literally sucks out every ounce of fat the mother has gained right out of her boobs. It makes her skinnier than she has ever been and ruins her once glorious rack. The only way that baby helps a father lose any weight is because every dad had to make the heartbreaking choice between diapers and tacos once in their life ... and diapers always win!

Morning Sickness:

Throughout our pregnancy, I worked the night shift. Pulling over to the side of the road to puke out the driver's side window on the way to work was such a usual occurrence for me that it would be unfair to blame this one on the Couvade. I have always been a puker, no matter what trimester I am in. So, we will just call this a wash. Megan found if she ate exactly 9 Cheez-its, first thing in the morning, then she would be fine.

Cramps:

Women in general complain about cramps so often that most men no longer pay attention to it. But take it from me, some night around the sixth month of pregnancy, you will be in one's bedroom, sound asleep, when you will wake up screaming because you had a charley horse worse than one ever had before. Your pregnant wife will run upstairs from her room (yes, we sleep in separate rooms. It started when I was on the night shift and I would go to sleep at 2 in the afternoon, but it continues because she snores and claims that I have a "jimmy leg." But, the real reason is that we are both selfish and fat and enjoy sleeping alone.) To check on you because she is concerned. Your leg will be on fire and she will offer such useless bits of information like, "Eat a banana." Like you are a god damned monkey! You will be in utter agony with tears running down your cheeks, and the woman who claims to love you, will offer you a piece of fruit! Might be best to just suck this one up and keep it to yourself...maybe keep your leather wallet next to your bed so you have something to bite down on until the pain subsides.

Breast Tenderness:

Oh, yeah. No joke. You're all in at this point. You'll
first notice it when your soul band is playing a show.
You and your sister Feowyn (the lead singer and star of
the show) are trying to get a Soul Train dance line
going in the crowd. You'll bust out the Running Man in
front of a room of 100 hot white girls, only to stop and
grab your own man titties. They hurt. You are 30 -years
old and should not be letting your boobs flop around
without a bra, like it's Woodstock for Christ sake! Have
some respect for yourself!

Sore Nipples:

One of the hardest parts of being pregnant is that your
wife's boobs will be bigger than they have ever been
before. They are very sensitive, so your wife won't let
you get within 40 yards of them for a solid year. You
will be jealous of your own son who is practically
living between those fun bags. But all of that pales in
comparison to how sensitive your own nipples will be.
Men's t-shirts, especially 20-year old men's t-shirts
with the Black Flag logo on them, are not made to
gently caress your raw, tender, pregnant man nips.
Everything you wear for the last month of your
pregnancy will make you feel like you are on mile 23 of
your first marathon.

Altered Hormone Levels:

I'm not a doctor, so I have no way of measuring how much testosterone I myself lost during the pregnancy, but I can assure you that it was a very emotional time for all of us.

Food cravings:

This probably goes along with what was covered in the weight gain section but having food cravings is normal for both the mother and the father. What is less normal is the need for Dad to eat a bowl of mint chocolate chip ice cream before bed every single night until the baby is fifteen years old.

And finally, Labor:

It is very common for women to evacuate everything from their bodies before they go into labor. Although I am not a woman, I was not pregnant, and I am not a doctor, I can only tell you exactly what happened to me when I went into labor. On our last pre-natal visit with the "Vagina Whisperer," Megan brought out the big guns. She started crying and told the doctor, "I can't. I can't do it. It's too fucking hot. I can't be pregnant for one more day. Get this kid out now!" The doctor took her polite request and scheduled a C-section for Wednesday morning. Since Megan's stripping career was mostly in her past, she was willing to take a C-section scar if it meant getting that kid out a week earlier. Wednesday was going to be perfect for us. Tuesday night we had special VIP passes to the grand opening of our friend, Matt Fish's, new restaurant, Melt Bar & Grilled. After being in bands with each other for years, it felt like both of us were having babies the same week. Plus, it would be nice for Megan and I to have one last date night before my son started cock blocking me for life.

When we got to melt in Lakewood, we were so excited for Matt. Everything looked so great. I had seen the bar that he bought a few months before the opening, and it was kind of a dump. Matt and his crew had put so much work into the place that it was hard to believe that it was the same old man bar I had seen before. Megan was extremely uncomfortable because she was so pregnant, but we forgot all about it when our food came. We knew it would be good, but we were blown away with how great it was. It was really nice to have a last dinner before doing this crazy thing together. We had a sweet talk and by the time we finished dinner, it felt like we were ready to meet this kid.

We said congratulations to Matt and then went to get some dessert at Malley's. Megan ordered an ice cream sundae and said, "Let's have a baby" as we toasted our water glasses. Not two minutes later, my stomach sent me a very urgent message: I needed to find a bathroom STAT! I excused myself and dropped some major league heat in the Malley's restroom. When I got back to our table, Megan said, "Are you ok? You don't look so good." I told her that I felt fine now, and we enjoyed our ice cream. Before we paid the check, my stomach exploded again. When I got out of the men's room, I told Megan something was wrong and we had to go home, right now.

I hit the freeway going about 140 mph and told Megan, "No matter what, you can never tell Matt that his new restaurant gave me food poisoning." Megan said, "I doubt very highly that you have food poisoning. I ate the same thing and I feel fine." Just then, another wave of nausea hit. I felt my stomach muscles tighten. It was a pain that I have not experienced ever before, or since. I wouldn't wish it upon John Elway or Billy Joel (I hate those fuckers). Megan stopped complaining about how fast I was driving and how I am an asshole for ruining her last night out long enough to say, "Lachlan? You are sweating. Are you ok?"

As soon as the pain started, it went away. I caught my breath and tried to regain my composure. The shooting pains came screaming back as we hit the off ramp. I ran 3 straight red lights to get home before I passed out. I parked the car on the front law n and ran toward s the bathroom. Megan yelled at me and I could feel her rolling her pregnant eyes at me, so I screamed, "I'm shitting my pants!!!" at her and just kept running. I made it to the bathroom in time. Barely.

By the time I got out of the bathroom, Megan had made it into the house to help me in to bed. I wasn't in bed for one full minute before I felt another contraction. I crawled to the bathroom; I was fully effaced. I was crowning. Megan told me that it was too late for me to get an epidural, so I had to tough it out.

To be honest, the rest of the night was a blur.

The next day my son, Declan, was born. It is true what they say: when you hold your newborn baby in your arms and look into his eyes, all the pain of labor just melts away...

The All Star

S ummer 1988 Cleveland, Ohio. Of all my years playing little league baseball this one was my favorite. I had really dedicated myself to the sport because I had to stay out of my house as much as possible. I was 12 years old, my parents divorced. My mother's boyfriend Gil moved into our house and I only spoke to my dad through sporadic letters. Girls weren't interested in me, so I spent a lot of time listening to AC-DC on my Walkman while I rode my bike around the neighborhood. Baseball season was a welcome distraction.

The season got off to a great start for me personally when instead of going door to door trying to sell candy bars like every other kid in the neighborhood, I made the very adult decision to save 50 bucks from my paper route and just buy the box of candy myself. This saved me the hassle of asking my mom for money later when I couldn't sell them and had the added bonus of giving me 50 candy bars to eat! It was what they call a Win-Win. The other highlight for me was that my cousin Ian had been picked for the same team. It was the first year we were able to be teammates and it was a blast. He was a pitcher. I was his catcher. He batted first. I batted second. Together, we made each other better. I always struggled as a hitter but this season was my best by far. Not only did I crack 300 with 2 homeruns (one was an inside the park deal that was aided by two errors) but because of our ages, most of the kids had gone through a big growth spurt, but because I was severely malnourished and my family didn't believe in vegetables I was still 4 foot 1 and a lean 87lbs! This meant that I easily led the league in walks! I had a good eye and would just let those other roided out pre-teen pitchers sail those pitches right over my head! It was the only time in my life I was happy to be a borderline little person.

During the second game of the season my mom and Gil may or may not have been killing a 12 pack in the bleachers and my mom's cheering (heckling) caused me to strike out three times. That night I put my foot down and banned them both from coming to any more games. I told my Mom that if I saw her at one of my games I would quit the team right then and there. Gil explained to my mom how all baseball players had superstitions and if this was mine then they should go along with it. If Wade Bogg's parents had to eat fried chicken before every game of his 20-year career then surely my mom could at least drink at my sister's games right?

It was a good thing that they honored my request to stay home because at the game the very next week I became the first 11- 1 4-year-old member of the North East Little League to be ejected from a game for calling the umpire a "blind motherfucker". In my defense, I had some anger issues about my parents' divorce and the umpire that day was Joe Frolik who was at least 96 years-old. There was a play at the plate and Mr. Frolik called this kid safe even though several inebriated parents sitting in the bleachers by right field could clearly see that I tagged him out easily 3 feet from the plate. I threw my helmet off and got real close to Mr. Frolik so I could show him and his Seeing Eye dog the ball that was in my glove when I tagged this kid! My coach came running out of the dugout in my defense, but when the Ump heard me question n his vision he threw me out of the game. I was forced to write an actual apology note to this old coot before I could play in another game. I sneezed on the note in the hopes that Mr. Frolik would catch something that would kill him but I am pretty sure he is still calling balls and strikes in braille up at Humphrey's field.

The rest of the season went pretty great. I loved playing catcher, I took it seriously and felt like a quarterback of the defense. I don't think it's a coincidence that my friend Charles was the MVP of the whole league and virtually unhittable with me behind the plate!

At the end of the season I was chosen with Charles, Ian and two other teammates to play in the all-star game I was pretty excited, I wasn't the best athlete in the world so this meant a lot to me. I wasn't even the best athlete in my family, my sister Bel was so good at softball she could have been a lesbian! Making an all-star team for her was expected, but it was a big deal for me.

My mother was furious that I wouldn't let her come to the game but no way was I gonna mess with that mojo. I told her she could come next year. When we got to the game the coach told us that Ian was gonna pitch the first three innings and Charles the last three. Ian was really nervous but I told him that it was just like playing catch in the backyard.

He walked the first batter on four straight pitches. I motioned for him to relax but he walked the second batter as well. I screamed, "COME ON!!" as I threw the ball back to the mound. He walked the third batter and I called time out and walked calmly out to the mound. I could see tears welling up in Ian's eyes as he realized that he just walked the bases loaded in his first ever all-star game. He would have gladly crawled in to a hole if given the opt ion, so as the veteran, older, calming voice of reason I was, I looked him in the eye and said, "IF YOU WALK ONE MORE GUY I AM GONNA BEAT THE FUCK OUT OF YOU AFTER TH E GAME!!"

I slammed the ball into his glove and walked back to the plate. We were down by 8 runs by the time we got out of the inning. Ian was shell-shocked the rest of the game. I wasn't exactly Johnny Bench out there and I have always felt bad at the way I acted. Part of me thinks that Ian's baseball career ended that day. Two summers later, he was listening to Metallica and growing a killer mullet. And there is no returning from that.

More News at Eleven

Back in the Halcyon days of 1996 when Megan and I had just moved in together, I was working for Safelite Auto Glass driving a delivery van. It was a pretty good job and one of the big perks was that I was alone all day in my van. My supervisor was a sweaty, depressed idiot named Bob. Bob was on my back all the time about going places or running errands in the van while I was on the clock. I would listen to him yell at me and then I would turn around and do whatever I wanted anyway. I was 20 years old and I knew how to read, I was pretty confident that I would get another job when he eventually fired me. That dude was so miserable all the time that I would sometimes chuckle when he would say stupid shit, "I've been writing down your mileage, so I know how often you are going out of your route!"

I would respond with something equally stupid like, "Well, if they would put a Taco Bell closer to my route we wouldn't have this problem!" His face would get beat red because he hated me personally but I was reliable and showed up to work every day. The truth about shit jobs like that is that they needed me way more than I needed them. And we both knew it.

So, on Valentine's Day in 1996, there was some kind of emergency and Bob needed me to run a windshield out to our Parma store. He made sure to tell me to "hurry up because we need the van back here for the next run."

After I delivered the part I heard a commercial for Malley's chocolates talking about how they have a drive thru line set up at their Brookpark location. I thought, "Well shit, Megan loves chocolate covered strawberries. I should go grab her a box!" I remembered Bob telling me to hurry back but the Malley's was just right down the road and I could hop right on the freeway. It will be easy as pie!

I pulled in to the Malley's and there was a pretty long line ahead of me but it was moving fast. After about 10 minutes I get to the front and place my order, as some kid runs in the store to get my stuff I notice this bitch Monica Robbins from Channel 3 News talking into the camera. The camera is very clearly pointing at me in my van and she is walking towards me.... The kid gets back and gives me my stuff just as Monica says into the camera, "Let's talk to someone..."

I hear her say "Excuse me, Sir" but I didn't get the rest because I hit the gas with both feet and tore the hell outta there!! That was all I needed was my asshole boss watching me on Live at Five while I was supposed to be making deliveries!

I never did find out if she was on the air live when I turfed her interview but more importantly either did Bob.

I told Megan how I risked my very livelihood to get her this gift but she was unimpressed. I showed her though because I am pretty sure that was the last Valentine's Day gift I ever got her!!!

Attempted Murder and Lessons Learned

I spoke to my attorney and he made me well aware of my rights regarding this story, but before we begin, I want you to know that it was an accident! When you are a kid you tend to do really stupid things in the name of fun.

Sometimes when you think back to ask yourself what you were thinking in the first place. For instance, once when we were young my parents had to go somewhere and left us kids without a baby sitter, which was no big deal because Warburton and Bel were with us (ages 12 and 9 respectively) and they were super responsible. Our family's washer and dryer were down in the basement and often we would just throw dirty clothes down the basement stairs. This was always a bone of contention with my dad who would get tired of tripping over an ever-growing pile of laundry at the bottom of the steps, safety always came first with my old man! My guess is as they were leaving that night my parents probably told us to collect all that laundry and move it to the laundry room where no one would trip over it. We were probably told to collect all the laundry from everyone's bedrooms and hampers too. I remember a giant pile of clothes dropping out of the sky from the attic and joining up with 3 bedrooms worth of dirty laundry in the hall. We kicked all those pants and sweaters and towels and socks and blankets and underwear and t-shirts down the kitchen stairs, around to the basement and then down the last flight of stairs until there was a laundry mountain 3 feet high!

When 4 children stare into the abyss of dirty school clothes there really was only one option before moving that pile into the laundry room. We wanted to jump into it from the basement stairs. All kids are looking for is a soft landing spot in life and maybe some candy. Once one kid made a laundry dive, the next kid was going to until all four kids were doing Greg Louganis impressions. Naturally, if I did a cannonball from step number 7, my sister Bel was gonna dive from step number 8 to prove her bravery until finally Warburton had to jump from the very top step because he is the oldest and the most accomplished stair diver in the whole family. After several rounds, our re-enactment of the 1984 summer Olympic Games was almost complete when Morrighan got caught up in a tangled web of smashed laundry and didn't get out of the way in time. Warburton performed what he later called "The 12th step swan dive" jumped before he should have and although the dive itself was absolutely graceful he botched the landing. Rather than the artistic belly flop that he had been perfecting all afternoon he chose to land with his knees up directly onto Morrighan's face. He received a lowly 5.5 from the East German judge and Morrighan was handed a broken nose. Luckily for Bel and me, the 4 quarts of blood pouring out of Morrighan's face were only staining Warburton's dirty clothes on top of the pile.

When our parents came home, we had to give them the news that our older brother just broke our younger sister's face and there was blood everywhere! Our parents asked, "What the hell were you idiots thinking?" We told them we were just having fun jumping off the stairs. That was a respectable answer. Even the most jaded adult can see the potential for fun in jumping into a pile of laundry!

Mo got her nose fixed up and if I remember correctly Warburton was the only one who got yelled at for the whole affair.

Or there was the time that Warburton and I were taking turns throwing a Styrofoam airplane outside. There were 2 long pieces of lightweight Styrofoam that would fit together so that it would resemble an airplane, then you waited for a windy day and you threw it. Sometimes it would catch a gust of wind and soar like an eagle but more often than not there would be no wind and it would fall out of the sky 4 feet away from where it took off. After a couple of good runs, small pieces of the plane broke off after each landing. Not great toys to begin with, they usually only cost a dollar or two because a child was really only guaranteed 10 or 15 minutes of enjoyable, quality playtime. These planes were sold at gas stations or drug stores because Kiddie City didn't have a section for "welfare toys." I had them throughout my childhood. It's probably because they fit into my father's definition of what an acceptable toy was- 1. It was cheap. 2. It could be shared. 3. It didn't require batteries. Those were 3 of his big checkmarks when buying something for us, the fact that it had to be used outside and it usually ended up in the garbage later that day so he didn't step on it at night were just looked on as a great bonus. Add in the fact that they were really no fun at all and you can understand why my dad couldn't help himself but to buy one when we were foolish enough to ask.

So, one afternoon while my brother and I are trying in vain to play with this trash heap toy our Uncle Tommy stopped over and watched our pitiful attempts at flight. Tommy probably came over to get high with my folks anyway so we could trust he was an expert at aero-dynamics. He threw the plane one time and then sent me in the house for some duct tape. He told Warburton to go grab a big rock under the tree. By this point all the kids on our street were very interested in what Captain Tom Sullen Berger had in store for us. Tommy taped the rock to the nose of the plane and said, "This should do it". He walked into the middle of the street and let it rip. The Styrofoam plane took off like it was built by NASA, it caught a gust of wind and soared in a beautiful line towards the heavens. I'll never know for sure, but I swear I saw a single tear running down Warburton's face. It was a thing of beauty the kind of flight that must have been what the Wright brothers envisioned all those years ago. Before my uncle Tommy could turn around and bask in the glory of impressing the under 12 population of Grovewood Avenue, the plane took a sudden and ill-advised hard left hand turn and sailed almost in slow motion directly into Mr. Porters living room window. Thank God Tom had the foresight to tape that big ass rock to the front of the plane so it shattered their picture window into a million tiny pieces! Without that weight on the front of it, the plane probably would have just bounced right off the window but because of Uncle Tommy's vision it was now resting on top of the Porter's television set. Obviously the sound of breaking glass sent 40 kids scattering in 40 different directions and poor Uncle Tommy stood silently in the middle of the street to take the full measure of Mr. Porter's anger. I heard our always angry neighbor screaming "YOU PEOPLE ARE ANIMALS! WHAT'S WRONG WITH YOU?" from inside the house before I set a new land speed record for the 40-yard sprint.

Tom gladly replaced the window that day and never forgave his shitty nephews for abandoning him when the shit hit the fan. When our parents asked about it we were able to say that we were just innocent bystanders in Tom Niedel's aviation adventures but again, every adult can understand what we were aiming for. The problem is when the adults look at the aftermath of a situation and just can't understand what you were even trying to do in the first place. Sometimes, the things that are the most fun make no sense.

Like the time Feowyn and I were playing some sort of tag while running around the dining room table. Even though she was only 5 and I was 12, together we should have realized that our game was both dangerous AND stupid. We would run at top speed around and around the table avoiding the 4 jagged corners of the table, avoid running into the piano on one side of the room and the buffet on the other while also making sure not to trip on various vacuum cleaner cords and accessories in one corner and the steel radiator in the other. You can probably see where this is headed right? We ran and laughed and to make the game more interesting every time one of us were tagged we would immediately change direction. Surely some parental figure should have put a stop to this game sooner but their whereabouts were unknown. I was It, so I chased Feowyn around the table a few times until I lunged and dove to get her, my hand hit her back with just enough force to send her flying face first into the side of the buffet. Her 5-year-old face smashed against a polished antique piece of furniture with all the momentum we could muster. I knew she was going to be hurt but when she turned to look at me I was wholly unprepared to see her face instantly covered in blood! I ran upstairs to get Bel or Warburton and get them to come help. Bel got Feowyn to calm down and put some ice on her head, but she had a 4-inch gash just above her right eyebrow. Warburton said that the cut was pretty deep and she would probably need stitches, so he and I hopped on our bikes to go ride around the bars to see if we could find Mom. I wish I could tell you that this was the first or the only time that I had to walk into a bar on E.156th to go find my mother and tell her that there was an emergency at home and she needed to sober up enough to drive someone to the hospital but that is just not the case.

I know you think the story ends with my mom passed out in the waiting room of a hospital, 13 years-old Bel holding Feowyn's hand as a doctor puts 30 stitches in her head but where is the drama in that?? No, I like for my stories to make you feel like you are listening to side 1 of Bruce Springsteen's Nebraska but with a better beat!

Feowyn, Bel, and my mom got home late that night. I felt terrible for Fe, it was a silly game we were playing and I never wanted her to get hurt. I apologized and even stayed home from school the next day to help cheer her up. Her eye was almost swollen shut and she was in a lot of pain so I just read her stories and tried to make her laugh to keep her mind off of it. She looked like a 5-year-old Rocky Balboa. After 2 or 3 days she started complaining about how bad it was still hurting and Bel and I were concerned that the swelling wasn't going down the way we thought it should. Mom asked us both how long we had been practicing medicine when we told her about our concerns. That night Feowyn couldn't get any sleep and in the morning, Bel took her temperature and she had a fever of like 128 or something. Bel convinced my mom that something was wrong so they went back to the hospital that morning. After a battery of tests were performed the doctors discovered that Feowyn had a staph infection. She was admitted on the spot and the doctors actually had to remove some of the stitches in her injury to replace them. Turned out that sending a 5-year-old with a gaping head wound home to a dirty house filled with 5 other kids and their friends, massive amounts of

cigarette and marijuana smoke, and less than ideal
bathroom conditions is a pretty good breeding ground
for infection. We older kids were immune because
thanks to our year round exposure to the elements
living inside the Grovewood estate we had developed a
highly specialized immune system, but the two younger
kids were sitting ducks for all sorts of viral intruders.

After the doctors replaced a few of the stitches above
her eye and cleaned her wound they put Feowyn on
antibiotics and kept her in the hospital for 5 days until
they were sure the staph infection had been neutralized.
I don't know if it is a lingering holdover from this
incident but Feowyn never again played a single game
of tag in her life! She ended up losing almost 20 lbs. as
a result of her hospital stay and staph infections kill
hundreds of people each year, they are nothing to mess
with. My mother made sure to include the phrase "she
could have died!" whenever she would talk about it to
me, so I know that at least Mom held me responsible
for the whole debacle, but to her credit Feowyn never
held it against me as far as I know. Even now whenever
I talk to Feowyn I take notice of the scar above her eye
and feel a twinge of guilt about it. Not a big twinge
though, that scar built character.

Hearing Impaired

After all those years of playing loud rock and roll shows in front of adoring female fans standing right in front of a 100-watt Marshall amp and Matt Fish's crash cymbal, it should come as no surprise that my hearing leaves a little to be desired. I am not deaf but I have often been told that the TV is on "way too loud", or if a bunch of people are talking at the same time I have trouble making heads or tails out of any of it.

After we bought our house in 2000, I set up my stereo in the basement and my favorite thing in the world to do was to put on a record, grab a book and relax in my little man cave. Megan was really cool about letting me have my alone time in the basement. She enjoyed it too because she would be upstairs vegging out watching episodes of Roseanne or Law and Order without me making my hilarious but annoying contributions. Since we lived in Euclid that meant that we had a Euclid sized house and our living room where she was watching TV sat directly above my man cave where I was listening to The Stooges and because I am deaf she would often have to come downstairs and ask me to turn it down.

This was no good for me. Not only do I want to hear every note that I am listening to I want to feel Scott Asheton's bass drum in my chest. I wasn't interested in background music. I was interested in surround sound music. Plus, we all know that some records are scientifically engineered to be played at maximum volume (Looking at you Black Sabbath) and not doing so is an insult to both the band who made the record and Science itself. Since I was not about to get myself on the wrong side of science the compromise that we made is that I would wear headphones if I needed the music to go above certain acceptable levels. And I did. The only drawback to this plan is that when I had headphones on I was incapable of hearing anything else, so if the phone rang or Megan called downstairs I would miss it. No one ever called for me on the phone anyway so it was really just a problem for Megan and a small one at that.

I was down in my office enjoying the second Grand Funk Railroad album and questioning the meaning of existence one day when half way through side one I could have sworn I heard a knocking at the door. I pulled my headphones off and looked up the stairs but No one was at the side door so I got back to the task at hand of rocking out with Mark, Don and Mel. Sure enough, I heard that pounding again so I took my headphones off a second time and waited...and waited...! I didn't hear anything else so I put the music back on. I figured it was probably just those kids next door playing basketball or something. Megan was upstairs, and if it was anything serious she would have come down.

I flipped the record over to side two and sat back down, before I could even find my place in the book I was reading my beautiful wife came charging down the stairs in sweat pants and a bra. Her hair was all mussed and she was sweating. I ripped off my headphones but before I could even ask her what's wrong? She started laying into me, "Are you fucking deaf?? You are kidding right? You didn't hear me pounding on the Goddamn floor upstairs!! ??"

She was pretty upset. I was gonna have to be very careful I thought to myself. As I went to answer, her tirade resumed, "I was choking to death on a fucking Advil, while you are down here scratching your balls! I had to give myself the motherfucking Heimlich maneuver by leaning myself against the bathtub like some kind of shut in or something!!! I didn't know what to say...I put my arms around her and gave her a hug, I could still feel her heart beating out of her chest. "I'm so sorry" I said. I tried in vain to explain to her that I had headphones on and I didn't hear anything. (Note to self: Never admit that I heard some weird pounding to her. Ever.)

In an effort to make her feel at ease I asked her if she still had a headache but that just made her slap me and march back upstairs. I followed her up to the living room and sat down with her. She eventually put a shirt on and calmed down but this is really not one of her favorite stories. She was less than enthusiastic when she heard me telling our friend Kerry about "The least excited I have ever been to see Megan come downstairs without a shirt on!"

I really did feel bad when it happened, I still feel bad about it. I think the moral of the story is that the next time you have to choose between saving the life of your one true love and listening to Grand Funk Railroad's ferocious second album there really is no wrong choice.

Honeymoon in Vegas

I have made many mistakes in my life, getting married at 22 was not one of them. I knew from the day we met that I wanted to spend the rest of my life with Megan. By the summer of 1998 we had already been together for 3 years, lived together for two, and been engaged for almost a year. We talked about having a wedding that August, we had some money saved up so we started to think about the logistics of a wedding. We had to pay for everything ourselves so I told her to make a list of the people she had to invite to a wedding, not second cousins or people she worked with but the absolute bare minimum of family and friends we could get away with. My list was 14 people and I was willing to cut 7 of them, her list was over 100. We quickly realized a wedding wasn't gonna be in our budget. All I could think about was my mother drinking the bar dry and my dad and Megan's dad getting into a fistfight over some political issue. The more we thought about it the more problems we envisioned and frankly, I'll be damned if I was going to blow my life's savings on buying dinner for those people! So I brought up the idea of just saying fuck it and eloping. Megan was on board!

Since it was just us, we were able to kind of treat ourselves and actually have a honeymoon. Megan booked us the honeymoon suite at the MGM Grand in Las Vegas and we decided to hang out in the desert in August because Irish people love extreme heat. It was my first time flying on an airplane and I was feeling like a big boy already! When we touched down in sin city the pilot let us know that it was a balmy 140 degrees in Las Vegas and our vacation was well underway! The room we stayed in was bigger than my house! Everything was fancy and top of the line, it was fun to pretend like we could afford this lifestyle for a couple days. Our first night in the hotel we learned the hard way that you should never pour bubble bath into a Jacuzzi unless you are trying to recreate the Rolling Stones It's Only Rock and Roll video but we didn't care, we had never seen so many bubbles!

The next day was our big wedding day. Megan had booked everything in advance and she spared no expense! She paid the extra 40 bucks so we could have the gold package at the Shalimar Wedding Chapel. Included in that package was a limousine that picked us up at the hotel and took us to the county courthouse where we filled out paperwork that stated to the best of our knowledge we were not already related or married to anyone else. The limo then drove us to the Shalamar Wedding Chapel where we got to have a quick meeting with our Elvis impersonator to pick out the 3 songs he would be performing for us. I'm telling you, the Gold package is a bargain! When the King of Rock and Roll suggested he sing Can't Help Falling in Love while he walks your future wife down the aisle, I didn't argue! Even though everybody knows I really prefer his early Sun Records singles, I went with it.

I stood at the altar with the minister and waited as Elvis Presley himself sang one of his sappiest songs ever while he walked Megan down the aisle. I was so happy I didn't even mind his left hand was clearly resting on Megan's butt. As they got up to the altar Megan started to cry a little, I was worried that she had come to her senses and was about to hop into Elvis's Cadillac and high tail it out of there but they were just tears of joy. The King kissed her on the cheek and said "Good luck y'all" and the minister began a short ceremony. Elvis belted out a fantastic version of Hunka Burnin Love as we exchanged our wedding bands. Next thing I knew I was told to kiss my bride and Elvis started ripping out Viva Las Vegas as a secretary threw rice at us. We were now married. Megan was on the fence about taking my last name but I told her that if I had to be a MacKinnon then so did she and she relented.

We tipped Elvis and he signed an 8x10 glossy photo of himself (included in the Gold package) and gave us our very first piece of marital advice. He said, "You kids should make love every single day!" and he moved on to the next couple who just arrived at the chapel. Even at 22 I thought that making love EVERY day seemed a little excessive but I sure as hell was not gonna argue with the King! We hopped in the limo and went back to our hotel room where either Elvis's advice or the overwhelming passion of the afternoon got the better of me and I decided that we had to consummate our marriage right then and there! 3 minutes later my annoyed wife got in the shower and started getting ready for our big night out. We were going to Caesar's Palace to see George Carlin perform! Some of you may think this is an odd way to celebrate your wedding night but the whole concept of marriage is sort of ridiculous and since George Carlin has always been a personal hero of mine it felt strangely fitting. Anyway, my dad said that the first two marriages don't even count. We had some time to kill before the show and since it was our wedding night I thought we should go to one of those fancy, expensive restaurants to celebrate but Megan suggested eating at the buffet here at the MGM. Since I am always a fan of the words all you can eat I decided to plunk down the 5.99 each for us to enjoy what the brochure in our hotel room called "the best deal in all of Las Vegas".

My new wife sat down with a very sensible plate of prime rib and almost sprained her neck rolling her eyes at me when she saw me walk back to the table with two plates overflowing with fresh shrimp!

"Baby, it's like they're just giving this shit away up there!!" I tried to explain to her.

"Lachlan, you are gonna get so sick if you eat that. The human body can only handle so much shellfish!"

My new wife obviously had a lot to learn about my abilities. I was adhering to the very strict Bill MacKinnon rules of buffet etiquette that clearly states that one must always skip over the salad bar to locate the most expensive piece of meat on the buffet and then eat large quantities of said item. It was jumbo shrimp that is a high dollar item. If I could eat two plates full then I would easily be making my money back and for the first time in my life making my father proud of me! I told her I could always go back for healthier options AFTER my dinner was paid for. I also reminded her when she rolled her eyes at me like that it gives me a boner. After I had eaten roughly 300 dollars' worth of delicious skrimps, we made our way over to hear the latest preachings from St. Carlin.

The show was fantastic, George came out on stage
wearing sweatpants and preceded to tell the crowd
that he doesn't give a shit about any of his Las Vegas
audiences because "most of you degenerate gamblers
were given comp tickets to the show because some
middle management dick wad decided to grow a heart
and he felt bad that you just lost your daughter's
college fund because you had a hunch, so he threw
you a bone and now I have to try to make you fuckin
laugh??" He said he used his Vegas dates as warm-
ups for "real shows with paying crowds." It was the
equivalent of a band opening up with a song called
"Fuck You" and it warmed my punk rock heart. He
did a solid 90 minutes of all new material and each bit
was killer!

Somewhere near the end of the set I started to feel a
gentle rumbling in my intestines and I started to do
that emergency math of trying to figure out if you
could hold your butt cheeks together long enough to
get to the hotel room or if you needed to find a
bathroom close by. When the show finished I told
Megan that I needed to go back to the hotel room and
she immediately gave me that silent look that most
wives have to be married for over a decade to pull off,
The look that says "You are a fucking idiot and I told
you not to jam all that shrimp into your pie hole!"
Megan had only been married for about 8 hours and
already she was a pro with those looks. I was both
proud and scared.

As I got up and walked around a little the severe
colonic pressure that was building began to subside,
we actually walked back to the room outside because
the air had cooled to a totally manageable 117
degrees. As soon as we hit the elevator my bubble
guts decided to crank it up a notch and I had to sprint
down the hall to the honeymoon suite. I made it to the
bathroom just a hair before the first bombs detonated
but my relief at NOT shitting my pants on my
wedding day was short lived when I realized that
those sons of bitches at that buffet had clearly
poisoned me with some kind of seafood ipecac that
was causing me to fire everything in my body out of
my butthole at the exact same time. It felt like I was
trying to pass a basketball and I seriously wondered if
the shrimp I ate earlier were still alive and trying to
escape my stomach any way they could. I have often
read where soldiers in combat can lose track of time
because of the intensity of the fighting and now knew
what they meant. I could have been in there for 10
minutes or 2 hours, I had no idea.

When I thought the battle was done I slowly walked
out of the destroyed luxury bathroom and went to see
if Megan had divorced me yet. She was sitting on a
couch in the east wing of our suite with a can of cold
ginger ale and a dose of Imodium waiting for me. She
had taken off her heels but she had not yet removed
her bra so there was still a small glimmer of hope that
we could salvage our night. I thanked her profusely as

I took the medicine and I promised that I would listen to her the next time we went to a buffet but we both knew that was a lie. She asked if I was feeling up to going back down to the casino for a little while but before I could answer her I had to run back to the bathroom for round two. I reached into my pocket and pulled out my wallet as I ran for the commode, I threw all the money I had on me at her and said "Help yourself! I'm gonna be awhile.... Please go, have fun, SAVE YOURSELF WHILE YOU STILL CAN, DAMNIT!! !" As the bathroom door slammed I saw her unhook her bra and shake her head.

People have a tendency to build things up in their head when they are excited about something and I'm sure Megan never pictured watching re-runs of ER while her husband assaults the sewers of the Las Vegas on her wedding night but that is what she got and she made the best of it. Together, we battled through the fire down below and we are a stronger couple because of it. I learned 3 very import ant lessons on my wedding night and because of what I learned I have been able to become Cleveland Ohio's most trusted marriage counselor (unlicensed).

Lesson number 1- Seafood at a buffet is almost always the wrong decision. -Take my word on this one.

Lesson number 2- A marriage is a marathon, not a sprint. - Even if you get a rough start you have to keep moving forward. You're in it for the long haul.

Lesson number 3- Setting the bar extremely low right from the start will only benefit you in the years that follow. - Not everyone is as charming as I am so not everyone can pull this off. You don't want to set the bar so low that your wife starts speed dialing divorce attorneys, but you do want to let her know what she is in for. In the 20 years since my wedding night every time I don't spend the evening in the shitter when we go somewhere is looked on as a great success and on the other hand, when we go out and I decide to start power eating tacos against her advice, well she's been through that already and she knows that she married an idiot so she can't get too upset.

And that, my friends is a classic Win-Win.

Grandma

The very first time I ever met Megan's Grandma she told me to "Just call me, Gramma" and gave me a big hug. At that time, I only dated Megan for a month or two and this made me feel a little weird and I didn't really know how to address her when Meg and I left the family get together later that night. She made a face and rolled her eyes if I pulled an Eddie Haskell and called her, Mrs. Buchanan. Her kids may think it was rude for me to call her Betty and I just wasn't comfortable calling her Grandma. I dealt with this every time I saw her that first year. I just made sure I looked directly at her when I spoke to her so I could avoid the whole issue.

My Grandma MacKinnon was a wonderful, sweet, caring woman who passed away when I was 14 years old. Most people in my family refer to her as a saint. When I got my first job at the grocery store across the street from the high rise where she lived, I would stop by her apartment to visit almost every Sunday. I am glad that I made the time to go see her but I don't know if I ever got to know her very well. I was still a kid and because of the way certain things were in my family there were a lot of things that her and I didn't talk about. I never got to know her as anything more than a grandma and when she died I remember kicking myself for not spending more time with her.

My grandma on my mother's side, Pauline died when I was 17 but I never really had much of a relationship with her. She and my mother had their own complicated issues and when we would see Grandma Pauline I always got the feeling that she didn't know what to do with us. She was always very sweet when we would go visit but her other grandchildren would tell her stories about golf tournaments or tennis lessons at the country club and we MacKinnon kids would tell her about cable finally coming to Collinwood and stories about cars breaking down. We grew up in a different world.

When Megan and I moved in together in 1996 it was right around the corner from her Grandma's house on E.157th Waterloo, so we would go visit grandma and do our laundry sometimes. I loved getting to know Betty, she was from the neighborhood, her kids went to the same school and church as us and her husband worked for the same company that my dad did. We had a lot in common, even with my dysfunctional family there was never anything you could bring up that she hadn't been through before. She could tell you the best way to deal with things and if she couldn't you would at least feel better after talking about it with her.

One day while I was on a delivery at my job I bent over and split my pants. I really did not want to deal with a bunch of warehouse dudes making fun of my fat ass hanging out of my pants for the rest of the day so on the way back to the warehouse I got off the freeway and stopped at Betty's. She was surprised to see me at 11 in the morning unannounced but she dropped what she was doing and started to sew my pants for me so I could get back to work. As I sat in her kitchen in my underwear, ate the lunch she made for herself but she INSISTED that I eat it instead and watched her sew up my blown out pants by hand I realized that I was more comfortable with her than I had ever been with my own grandparents and I told her this. She just laughed and said "That's because I AM your grandma now!"

When you fall in love and get married you inherit your partner's families and if you have been together as long as Megan and I have, that family becomes your family. Her aunts are my aunts, her uncles are my uncles and her Grandma sure as hell is my Grandma. My grandma died since and a little part of my heart will never be the same. I love you, Gram.

The Funeral Suit

O f all the traumatic things that a person has to go through when one's mother dies, what you wear to the funeral would probably rank pretty low on the list. Maybe it tells you more about me and my own issues, buying a suit to wear to my mother's funeral was my own personal Vietnam.

When my mom finally succumbed to the leukemia that poisoned her from the inside, it came as a shock. She was sick for quite some time and doctors made it clear she was never going to get better. I visited her and gave her one last hug. It was a big deal for me because our relationship was so terrible it was the first and only time I went to see her for the last year of her life. My siblings and my wife visited her and gave me reports about how she was doing. I was still so angry and stubborn that I just did not want anything to do with her. My thinking was because she was sick it did not erase everything she did for the previous 5 years. Honestly, I buried my mother in my mind a long, long time before she ever died.

When I got the phone call from my sister she died, it was kind of a relief. I was glad she was no longer in pain and we kids could move forward with our lives. That was 18 years ago now and here I am writing this...We all move forward at different speeds.

When someone dies there are so many things to be done. Bel, Morrighan and I were busy. Bel took care of the lion's share of planning as usual but she delegated enough so that no one was overwhelmed. Once everything was set up as far as the wake and funeral go it dawned on me I didn't really own too many nice outfits, 23 year old punk rock warehouse employees don't normally have many occasions to be dressed up for.

Megan calmly explained to me that no, I could not "rent a suit at a mall or something" and I was an adult man and owning a suit was probably a wise investment. People die. People marry. People go to court. It was not out of the realm of possibilities to think I would wear a suit more than once. I reluctantly agreed with her but you guys know how I feel about spending money. Especially on clothes... I was not happy.

We went to a clothing store that was not in a mall and I followed my wife like a pouting kid. I looked at a couple price tags and immediately tried to get out, but

Megan (wisely) held my hand and lead me to the suit section. She calmly explained to the sales men what we were looking for and before I knew it some fake-ass George Zimmer is measured my inseam and asked me to take off my hoodie.

Megan and the sales man talked some more about what style and the sales man talked some more about what style and the occasion this suit was for. By this point my eyes glazed over and I no longer had any opinion on the matter. She could have bought me a purple tuxedo at Mr. Alberts and I would not have cared as long as I got it over with as fast as possible.

The salesman offered his condolences to me and said that he knew just what we needed I smiled halfheartedly and followed him down a long row of black suits. As we walked I focused on large cardboard placards hung from the ceiling and started to worry. We walked past Large and Extra Large into a section marked Husky. My heart started pounding as I looked up at the next section, Portly. Please God do not let me be portly, please! I sweated as we were deep into the husky section, the salesman was fingered through jackets looking at sizes and I was seriously questioned my decision to never go on a diet in 23 years! I knew I was not in tip-top shape but I never thought I was portly! And P.S. What year was it that the word Portly was acceptable to use in public anyway? And what comes after Portly? Ample, f-ig, Obese? Why not just have a rack of MuMus and a big sign that says Fat Ass!

"Here we are!" said the salesman and pulled out a nice suit for me to try on. I didn't even care, it was still clearly in the husky section so I quickly said, "SOLD" and tried to run out of there! Megan made me try it on and she picked out some shoes for me. The husky suit looked nice on me and for exactly one minute I forgot why I was buying it in the first place.

I've worn that same suit a hundred times in the past 18 years. It still fits and more importantly it makes me smile when I think of the day I bought it. If focusing on my humiliation was how I got through my mom's funeral than that suit did a lot more than just make me look presentable that day. Over time all the anger and stubbornness I felt towards my mom faded away. When I think about her, I think of the good times. She would have told me how handsome I was in that suit and she would have laughed at me being so angry about buying it.

Enjoy your mom. You will miss her when she is gone, I guarantee it.

My Son, the Superhero

Being a parent is a weird gig. You could do absolutely everything right and your kids could still turn out to be dicks. Or you could be the worst kind of absentee, borderline abusive parent and your kids will overcome it all to be perfectly well adjusted adults, like all 3 of my sisters. The really hard part is that you just don't ever know. Sometimes if you're lucky you get small glimpses of your children doing the right thing and it puts a smile on your face.

Like this one time at my sister BelPhoebe's house, her daughter Ella came in the house told a story about how some kids down the street called her names and without even thinking my son Declan threw down his video game and said, "Where? Show me." and ran out the door like he was gonna go kill those kids! We stopped him, but I was proud his first reaction was kick some ass to protect his cousin! It was some true Collinwood attitude running through him!

When I think about being proud of my only son I will always think about a time when he really did save the day! For the first 8 years of his life I worked the night shift and would come home and hang out with him all day. It was hard on me but I loved every minute of it. A few times a week we would have to go and do something so I wouldn't fall asleep on the couch. When he was about 5 years old we went to Chuck E Cheese to play some video games. They opened early and we usually had the place to ourselves. Declan could burn through tokens playing Star Wars and it was loud enough that it would keep me awake! It was a win-win.

We made our rounds and played games when a single mother and her two year-old son started yelling at each other. Declan was pretty oblivious but I could tell that the mother was getting more and more upset.

As we walked by them I calmly asked the woman, "Are you ok?" and she smiled and explained that her son had crawled up into those weird jungle gym type tunnels suspended from the ceiling and he was crying because he couldn't figure a way out. I told her that I would be happy to help but there was no way that my fat ass could crawl through the maze to where he was. I gotta believe that I was at least a hundred pounds over the weight limit.

So I turned to Declan and said " Hey can you crawl up there and show that kid how to get out?"

"No thanks, I don't like it in there" he said and turned back to his game. Clearly I would need to take a different approach...

"Declan, What do you want to be when you grow up?"

"Batman."

"Right, and what is Batman?"

"A superhero.....so?"

"So right now is your chance to be a hero and help someone in trouble! Just crawl up there and show this kid where the slide is. He will follow you."

Once he realized it was no longer just training, Declan ran up the ladder to put an end to this baby Jessica situation. He crawled through the maze to where the boy was stuck, got him to turn around and he followed Declan to the slide. Both kids were sitting at the top of the slide. We could see them but we couldn't reach them. The boy was REALLY crying now because he was scared to go down the slide and his mother was one step away from getting hysterical!

She bent over reached up the slide as far as she could but the kid wouldn't budge. I stood behind her where she couldn't see me and I motioned for Declan to push the kid. Declan smiled, gave me a thumbs up and pushed this little crying shit right down that slide!!

The Mother burst into tears hugging and yelling at her son. Declan and I went back to our table to finish our lunch. The woman bought us ice cream and thanked Declan profusely. He acted like it was no big deal, just another average super hero lunch for my dude!

As much as I enjoy working days now, I do sometimes miss our daytime adventures! I love that kid!!

Collinwood SVU

Dateline: Cleveland Ohio, June 1982

Today Police were called to the 1500 block of Grovewood Avenue in the North Collinwood neighborhood in what witnesses are calling "A close call with tragedy." Shortly, before 6 pm, neighbors reported children's screams coming from the backseat of a 1977 Volkswagen Rabbit that had rolled down the driveway of Bill MacKinnon's and into oncoming traffic.

An officer on the scene explained, "After a thorough investigation we determined an argument between the children about radio stations led to several different suspects reaching up from the back seat to change the station. As of now, no one is admitting guilt but we suspect during the horseplay described, someone most likely bumped the stick shift and knocked it from PARK to NEUTRAL. At which time the car rolled down the driveway of the MacKinnon residence into the Hurtack driveway directly across the street, then back down the Hurtack driveway before coming to a stop in the middle of Grovewood."

When reached for comment, oldest brother Warburton MacKinnon age 11 said, "Look, when you hear the

opening riff to Aqualung by Jethro Tull, you DO
NOT change the station, You crank the volume!!"

Sister Belphoebe MacKinnon age 8, replied "Last
time I checked this was still America and we voted 3-
1 to listen to PYT by Michael Jackson. We cannot be
held accountable to the fact that our older brother
doesn't believe in democracy!"

When paramedics arrived on the scene 6 year old
Lachlan MacKinnon was treated for symptoms of
shock and fatigue, remarking to the attending EMT "it
was like slow motion, I saw my whole life flash
before my eyes..." Although no serious injuries were
reported, youngest sibling Morrighan MacKinnon
was given several lozenges to treat her sore throat due
to massive, uncontrollable screaming and crying.
Doctors advised both younger children be kept under
strict observation for the remainder of the weekend.

The authorities then turned the investigation towards
the parents to find out why 4 children were left alone
in a hot car with no adults. After questioning both
adults separately, it was determined the mother and
father told the kids to get in the car because they were
going out to eat. The parents stayed behind for less
than 5 minutes so they could "build their appetites"
before leaving. Detectives have been looking into
what "building your appetite" entails but did note in
the report that there was secondary evidence of

possible marijuana use in the house including a "strong aroma of recently burned Collinwood Ditch Weed".

At this time no charges have been filed although police noted patriarch Bill MacKinnon age 37 was "extremely uncooperative". He refused to speak to the police about the incident saying to a reporter "Talk to my lawyer" was later heard yelling at the four scared children about touching his radio and "fuckin with my levels." That would seem to imply battles over car stereo issues have been an ongoing situation.

Before leaving the scene a witnessing neighbor who asked his identity be kept hidden said, "Thank God no one was hurt....That mother has her hands full, those kids are a constant problem on that side of the street....and is she pregnant again? Good Lord!!!"

The children were released to their parents at the conclusion of the investigation where they proceeded to a nearby York Steak House buffet where locals overheard Bill MacKinnon saying, "I'm not even fucking hungry anymore."

The Love Shack

Mother's Day bums me out. May 12 of 1999 was the date my Mother passed away and every few years it will fall on Mother's Day as an extra turn of the screw for my psyche, So I try to focus on more positive things when that day is coming up. May 12 of 1996 was the day that Meg and I moved in together and the following story is one that makes me laugh when I think about it and it also proves that I have pretty much always been an Asshole. A loveable, sometimes charming asshole! But an asshole nonetheless.

In 1996, I had been dating Megan for about a year and things were going well as far as our relationship went. She was living with her father at the time and he just moved to Rocky River, which was way too far west for anyone involved. I was still living at home in Collinwood but things at my house were pretty tenable so I spent as little time there as I could. We were not really even talking about moving in together but I had looked at a few apartments for myself and everything seemed out of my price range. As horrible as things were at my Mom's, it was free.... My older sister Bel had been living with her boyfriend Bill in a duplex just over the hill in South Collinwood. Bill joined the Army and Bel was going to move in with a friend to save money for school, so I asked to talk to her landlord about me taking her place.

Just between you and me, I think that Mr. Orlosky was so happy to have a white guy want to move in that he took Bel's word that I was reliable and never bothered to run my non-existent credit. I was gonna need a roommate to help cover the bills and thankfully Megan agreed before I had to ask any of my d-bag friends. She hated living on the west side as much as I hated going over there every weekend so as soon as Bel moved out, we moved in.

Living together was pretty great. There were all of those little adjustments to make and seeing as how I was raised by wolves it was admittedly much harder on Meg. She had to teach me basic human being coping mechanisms I missed out on in the wild. Things like sheets go on a bed before blankets, perishable food should be stored in a refrigerator and no one files their record collection geographically (a system that made perfect sense to me). The only drawback to living together was her mom lived in the same neighborhood and was a big fan of just stopping by unannounced.

Now, I loved Meg's mom (still do) and we got along great but I was always thrown off by her pop-ins. It was the 90's, why didn't she at least call us and give us a head's up?? I brought this up to Meg and she said that she would talk to her Mom about it. I really don't even know why it bothered me so much. I think it was because there were always so many people coming and going through my mom's house that I just wanted some privacy for once. It's not like Barb was coming over in the middle of the night and when she came over it was usually to do something helpful. She would bring us dinner or she would find something we needed at a garage sale and drop it off. Whatever it was I found it to be annoying. So I had to put a stop to it.

Megan and I had different schedules at the time. I would get home from work around 7pm but she was working as a server at a fancy restaurant and wouldn't get home until after midnight. So there I was sitting around in my underwear listening to records when the doorbell rang.

Rather than find my pants, I just walked down to answer the door in my boxers. I think I was wearing a t-shirt but I don't really remember. I opened the door for Barb, the only unexpected visitor we ever had. I invited her in. We sat down in the living room and talked. Then she asked, "Lachlan, do you want to go put on some pants?" And without missing a beat, I told her, "See Barb, Here's the thing. When I come home from a long hard day of work. I take a shower and then I like to sit around in my underwear. That's what I do. Now if you called and said you were gonna drop in, then I would have already put my pants on. But since you didn't call, here we are." My future mother in law was not amused.

"And while we're on the subject Barb, do you remember when you first moved in with your boyfriend? You probably don't, but let me tell you what goes on around here . See Barb, I am madly in love with your daughter. I can hardly keep my hands off of her. And I am worried one day you are gonna pop in and see us naked doing what a twenty year old couple does. Do you really want to see us banging? Cuz, that's what we do. A lot. All the time. Hell, that's why I don't bother putting pants on!!"

My future Mother in law grabbed her purse, apologized and left. I didn't think it was really that big of a deal until a few weeks later and Megan asked "I wonder why my mom never comes over anymore?"

Luckily, cell phones became more commonplace around this time so we started to get phone calls from Barb saying" Hi, I'm in your driveway, can I come up???" To which I would say "Well sure, let me put some pants on and I'll open the door."

That was the one and only time I have ever had any kind of argument or disagreement with Barb. She really is the best mother-in-law a guy could ask for.

I should have had this same conversation with my brother Malcolm before he walked in on Megan naked later that same summer!

And Still Champion!

W hen I was a kid, professional wrestling was a big deal to me. It was the early 80's and I was the perfect age to get caught up in the hype. Weekend mornings were scheduled around the different wrestling shows and due to some "creative" billing measures my father showed me I ended up with a long-running and never paid for a subscription to Pro Wrestling Illustrated. It was a glorious time!

As I got older I lost interest in wrestling. I got sucked back in after my Mom's boyfriend Gil moved in because he was a big fan. Gil and I didn't get along great but one thing that we could talk about was how cheesy and boring wrestling had become. We would actually talk about great matches from years earlier and would forget we didn't get along for a few minutes.

The early 90's were a bad time for professional wrestling and as a result ticket prices to the live shows got real cheap. One Friday night when I got home from school Gil asked me if I wanted to go to the Convocation Center at CSU to see wrestling with him and my brother Malcolm. Tickets were less than 10 bucks and Ric Flair was gonna be wrestling, I quickly checked my non-existent social calendar and said, "Sure".

I had seen a few wrestling shows before, my Dad took my friend Joe along with the rest of us kids to see the very first WWF Survivor Series at Richfield Coliseum when I was 10 or 11 but we sat in the nosebleeds. There was such a sparse crowd on this particular Friday night that we were able to get really good seats, maybe 6 or 7 rows from the ring. It was pretty cool! We were close enough to hear the slaps connect and the wrestlers gave dirty looks to hecklers (my specialty). When the wrestlers made their entrances to the ring we were close enough to touch them. I told Malcolm that the next guy who walked down our aisle, I was gonna punch them. Malcolm was only 5 so he hadn't yet figured out that his older brother was a complete moron, so he encouraged me to try to punch the next roided out head case that walked down the aisle.

The next wrestler that came towards us was Abdullah the Butcher. The MadMan of the Sudan. He was a 400 lb. black guy in his 60s whose whole claim to fame was he taped razor blades to his finger s and sliced up his opponents. I was a shit talking 15 year old idiot who was now gonna try to punch this guy to make a 5 year old laugh... I was more brave than smart so when Abdullah was within distance, I extended my arm like I was gonna give him five but at the last minute I slapped his chest as hard as I could. Abby whipped around with cat like reflexes and let out a giant yell as he lunged against the barrier where we were standing. I took off running so fast that I think I stepped on Malcolm's head! Gil and Malcolm were dying with laughter at how scared I was but fuck them. A Sudanese butcher was coming after me! Abdullah apparently smiled and just kept walking to the ring while I wet my pants in fear. I was bound to redeem myself somehow. All through the next match Gil was cracking on me about it. Every wrestler announced Gil dared me to slap him! I told him that I was "picking my moment" but the truth was that Abdullah was the only guy I could outrun!

Gil and I both talked about how much we hated the next wrestler. Lex Luger was everything that was wrong with wrestling. He was a steroid using body builder known as "The Total Package" but in truth he had next to no wrestling ability and his promos would put you to sleep. I didn't care about muscles, I liked the scrappy guys who were funny on the mic. Give me Ric Flair or Rowdy Roddy Piper over a chump like Luger or Hulk Hogan any day of the week!

As Lex walked down the aisle closest to us I picked up Malcolm's half eaten bucket of popcorn and I chucked it right at him. It was a direct hit to the side of his head and the crowd went nuts Lex Luger yelled at me to "Fuck Off" but before I could respond I was assaulted by security and dragged out of my seat. Gil threw me the keys to his jeep as the security guard led me down the same aisle that Sexy Lexi just came through. The crowd was still cheering for me as Barry Windham was announced and ran past me and the security guard.

I was pulled through the curtain backstage and I started to suspect that maybe wrestling wasn't on the level when I saw Nikita Koloff and Arn Anderson discuss the match they'd be having next. Why would a known bad guy like The Enforcer Arn Anderson be smiling and talking to that Russian baby faced punk?? Had I been lied to all these years??

Before I could get any answers we had reached the exit door and the security guard tossed me into the loading dock like a piece of trash. I walked around the arena to the lot where Gil had parked the jeep and I hopped into the back seat.

There was an older black guy hanging out on the corner of the lot who saw me go into the jeep and he kept looking around and then looked back at me sitting in the Jeep. I felt sketch sitting in a car in a dark parking lot with a bum/vagrant/crackhead/hobo casing the situation. Sure enough, the guy walked over to the Jeep just as I got out and walked away. He said, "Hey Man, I need a couple bucks". I said very politely, "I'm sorry, but I don't have any" at that point he opened up his jacket to show me the small gun. He pointed at me and he said, "I need some money." I reached into my pocket and handed him a 5 spot, the only thing I had. He took off walk in the other direction. I wasn't really scared at all, I was relieved he didn't ask for Gil's car keys in my other pocket. To be honest I was more scared of Abdullah the Butcher earlier.

I didn't want to go back to the parking lot where I was a sitting duck but I also didn't want to just hang out on Prospect Avenue so I walked back toward the arena. I walked right up to the entrance and the door wasn't locked to my surprise. I walked right back to my seat where Gil started laughing again and Malcolm asked if I was Batman! I only missed one match, I was back just in time to see Ric Flair defend his heavyweight championship against Ricky Morton.

On the way out of the arena after the match I told Gil that I had been robbed of the 5 dollars. He asked if I wanted to go make a police report but he was pretty hammered by this point and I was kind of worried that if we went to the police station the cops wouldn't let him drive home. I told him that 5 bux was a small price to pay to blast Lex Luger with that bucket of popcorn. We laughed and headed home. We never told my mom about any of it.

Obstinate

I think I read somewhere that stubbornness is a pretty common Celtic trait, certainly one that the MacKinnon family had in spades. When I was 8 years old I made the mistake of telling my dad that I was "bored", after giving me a six hour lecture explaining that only boring people are bored, my dad gave me 50 suggestions of things to do. When nothing on his list sounded like fun to me he threw up his hand s in defeat and said "Go outside and dig a hole or something" I knew that he wasn't being serious but all of a sudden the thought of digging a hole sounded fun to me. I went in the backyard and started to dig a hole.

In a classic Tom Sawyer move, I sold my friends on the idea of helping me dig a hole in my backyard too. By the end of the day the hole was starting to show some real promise. For the next two weeks digging became a pretty serious endeavor among the under 10 set on Grovewood.

My father was not an ideal landscaper when I was a kid, after 3 weeks of solid digging, Dad decided to mow the lawn in the backyard. Imagine his surprise when he came across a five-foot deep hole with his youngest son in the bottom of it!

"What the fuck are you doing?" He shouted at me, I calmly reminded him that he told me to go "dig a hole or something" a few weeks back and so that's what I have been working on all summer. Rather than argue with a kid standing 5 feet underground, Dad realized he now had a third less backyard to mow so he just laughed and called me an "idiot" and continued on with his chores. I think secretly he was glad that I finally did something he told me to do.

That hole in the backyard became a cool neighborhood hangout for my friends and me. Because it was impossible to get in and out of without getting really dirty the hole had the added benefit of being a boys' only club because no girl wanted to get filthy climbing in or out of it. One day, I threw a folding chair into the hole so I could enjoy reading my Encyclopedia Brown stories with the added comfort of not sitting on dirt. The hole was turning into a regular luxury bachelor pad.

Then the rains came. In August it rained hard for about 3 days straight. My new cool hang out was instantly turned in to a giant muddy toilet. I'm not sure if the hole ever completely dried out? There was about half a foot of gross standing water at the bottom of the hole and I learned the hard way that once your Nikes got waterlogged it became impossible to get back out of the hole because each step you took to climb up the side turned the dirt to mud and your eight year old feet would just start to slide back down the side of the hole.

The hole in the backyard t hen became a death trap that was to be avoided at all costs. The standing water at the bottom became a breeding ground for giant creepy crawly bugs not seen since the end of the conflict in Vietnam. The days were numbered for the hole when another rainy day contributed to a small landslide along the western half of the hole. The landside had contributed to Mr. Porter's new privacy fence starting to bow down and become less than stable.

Dad told me to "fill the goddamned hole" after a contentious discussion regarding the fence with Mr. Porter. None of my friends who helped dig the hole were very interested in now helping me fill the hole back in so I had to do it myself one shovel full at a time. It was like burying a friend.

The hole eventually got filled in but there was always a noticeable dip in the land where the hole was and grass never actually grew over it. That bald patch of dirt in my backyard came to represent childhood stubbornness in all its glory.

Bill MacKinnon's Greatest Hits!

The very first time Dad ever met Megan when we first started dating, he stole all 4 steak knives from the restaurant table where we were having dinner because, "These knives are fuckin' solid!"

If you were to ask Dad what his proudest accomplishment was he would gladly tell you that even though he has smoked pot every single day since 1963, he has never failed a drug test.

My dad does not have racist views at all, yet he refuses to eat Mexican or Chinese food because "That is peasant food."

When I was 15, I had already discovered punk rock, so I acted like I hated all other music. My dad made me go see the Grateful Dead with him, even though I hated them (still do). Right before the show started, he handed me a small piece of paper and said, "Here. Eat this."

I said, "I'm not taking LSD with you!!!"

"Don't be a pussy; it's a half... "

It was a pretty good show.

Dad discovered kayaking in his mid-fifties and took it up with a passion. He took me out kayaking around the Three Rivers of Pittsburgh once. We took a break near a pier where a bunch of women had just finished a yoga class. Dad couldn't resist flirting with a couple of the ladies. One woman said, "Hey. You should take me for a ride in that kayak sometime."

Instead of being nice to her and explaining that kayaks are made for one person at a time, he lit a cigarette and said, "Boy, are you stupid!" and we paddled away...

My father claims to have invented the Atkins Diet in 1970. He has not eaten a vegetable in 58 years.

I was once on a road trip with my dad and had fallen asleep in the car at night. He woke me up and said, "Hey. Can you drive for a little bit?" We switched seats and got back on the road. Suddenly, he put on a Stones tape and cranked the volume. "I thought you needed me to drive so you could sleep?" I asked. "No way. I think I'm havin' an acid flashback... I wanna enjoy this!" He played "Beggars Banquet" four times in a row.

My dad wore a black arm band for months after the siege at Waco. When people asked him who died, he answered, "America."

I'm 100% sure that my dad fell asleep standing up at a Neil young concert in the 90s.

My father once bought a house in Pittsburgh after he and my mom divorced. He only lived in this house for a few months before it caught fire and burned down. He still refers to this event as, "The best investment I ever made."

My Grandma MacKinnon was one of the sweetest people who ever lived. After she passed away, I was talking to Dad about her. Her maiden name was Yurko. I asked my dad how come he never admits being Slovenian. He said, I'm not. She was."

I have very few good memories of Christmas. But one Christmas Eve, when I was really little, I remember my dad singing along to Bruce Springsteen' s version of " Santa Claus is Coming to Town." He was singing at the top of his lungs in his scary, raspy voice, while doing doughnuts in his car. My brother, sisters, and I were flying around in the backseat while my mom was yelling at him to stop. My dad had the biggest smile on his face (he was obviously stoned), and it was snowing really heavy.

Dad later told me that Santa isn't real and that life is mostly bullshit.

The first summer that "The Wave" was open at Geauga Lake, my dad took us there. Some teenager who worked there said, "I'm sorry sir, but we can't allow you to go into The Wave wearing cut-offs." My dad laughed and said," Bullshit" and walked right on in.

Once time while visiting my dad in West Virginia, we all played a game of Scrabble. I am 40 years-old and for the very first time in my entire life I beat my dad!!!! It was one of the proudest moments of my life. I beat him by 90 points! As I was grabbing the scorecard, so that I could take it home for framing, I saw that he gave everyone but himself a 100 point head start. Even though it was the game of my life, I didn't beat him by 90 points; I *lost* by 10! That is the goddamned story of my life.

My dad once invited Jehovah's Witnesses into our house to talk. He asked this sweet, old lady if she wanted to get high.

My dad was living in Atlanta when my band the Chargers Street Gang came through town on a tour. We stayed with him that night at his house. After we played our set, we stayed at the club to watch the other bands play, but Dad went back home because he had work in the morning. He asked me if we were hungry when we got back. He said he'd grab us a snack. When we got back to his house later, he had bought us 6 dozen doughnuts! 72 doughnuts for 5 people. "Well, I wasn't sure what kind you guys liked."

Once when discussing how many times he had been married, my dad tried to convince Megan and I that the first one didn't count because he never had children with her. "There were no issues."

When Megan and I first moved in together, Dad came and stayed with us for a weekend. Our TV's volume went from 1 to 50. He put on "Jesus Christ Superstar" and turned the volume all the way up. Megan asked if he could tum it down a little. He said, "You're right; 49 really is the right number."

When we had to tell Dad his grandson had a severe gluten allergy, he said, "See. I told you that shit will kill you."

I was the first of Dad's 6 children to get married. As a gift, he gave me five hundred generous dollars. In singles. Wrapped in a shoebox. Two years later, when my sister got married, she got the gift...in quarters.

Dad always loved the movie "Overboard," with Goldie Hawn. It never made sense to me, until Megan pointed out it out: "Of course he does! That movie is about a guy who finds some rich lady and tricks her into taking care of his hooligan children! It's your dad's ultimate dream!!!"

When I was 19, I asked my dad if he would co-sign on a car loan for me. I already had a car picked out. When we went to the dealership, my dad told the sales man his real name so he said to me, "Sorry, but we have to go somewhere else. I can't risk messing with my real credit score. I am not co-signing for you...this guy is." He then showed me a driver's license under an alias!

"This guy has GREAT credit!

Showtime

When I was younger I was a fanatic about sports and my favorite non-Cleveland athlete was Magic Johnson. The Cavs played way the fuck down in Richfield at a Coliseum in between a cornfield and fishing hole in hillbilly land so I was never able to see a game in person. When I was 13 the Cavs were actually playing meaningful basketball late in the season and I saw that the Lakers were coming to town on a Friday night. It was also the last time that Kareem Abdul-Jabbar was gonna play in Cleveland so I devised a plan, I was gonna be at the game! My cousin Ian was in on the plan with me. We bought tickets in advance and started to get to work on figuring out how to get to Richfield.

We told Ian's mom that I got the tickets for free because I won them at school. I don't remember why we figured out that getting the tickets for free was a really important lie to try to pass off, probably because our parents were so cheap they wouldn't let a freebie go to waste, so they'd have to drive us! We also told my Aunt Micki that all she had to do was drive one way and my mom would drive the other. We lied and told her my mom already agreed. Of course, she had not.

Micki didn't want to be the bad guy so she reluctantly offered to drive the two of us down to Richfield. But she wanted us to know that she wasn't happy about it. We explained to my mom Ian won free tickets from school and Aunt Micki was gonna drive us down there, all she had to do was pick us up after the game. No big deal. She agreed and even wrote the date on the calendar. I was super excited! This was pre-HIV Magic Johnson and the Showtime Lakers against an actual playoff contending Cavaliers team!

The Friday of the game rolled around and we were so excited. Our Nerf hoop games got a lot more heated waiting for the day. We rolled down to Richfield with Aunt Micki complaining about the rush hour traffic the whole way. She gave Ian a five spot as she dropped us off at the front entrance. The game was everything we hoped for. The Lakers won a nail biter that actually came down to Byron Scott hitting a three-pointer with less than a minute left to win. Our seats were terrible, but we didn't care. It was such a cool atmosphere. I still think that basketball games are the best sport to see in person. After the game, we joined the crowd and filed out of the arena.

We told my mom we would be at Gate A as soon as the game ended. We waited there. And waited…

After about an hour, we started to worry. Most of the crowd dissipated and I did a lap around the arena to see if she was at another gate. She wasn't. I pulled an emergency quarter out of my pocket to call home. My older brother answered the phone. "Hey Warburton, is Mom there?"

My brother assessed the desperation in my voice and said, "No, I'm on the other line!" and hung up. What an asshole! It was my last quarter!

While we waited, we watched two older black guys trick drunk suburbanites into playing Three Card Monte. By my count, they must've made about $8000 before a security guard chased them off.

The security guard asked us what we were waiting for and when I explained that my mom was running a little late he laughed and told us to be careful and to watch out for parking lot ghosts. What kind of dick would say that to two scared kids anyway?! We were from Collinwood, so ghosts didn't bother us but we figured there were definitely Children of the Corn down here watching our every move.

The game had been over for 2 hours and the parking lot was empty. It was after 11pm. All the employees were gone for the night. I asked Ian if we should call his mom and Ian said, "I would rather live in this parking lot for the rest of my life before I would call her!" So that was out... We started to logically think if we could hitch-hike home, but we decided to stay where the light was on.

Ian went to gather wood for a parking lot fire and I made a collect call to my house that no one picked up.

Then we heard a familiar muffler and started running toward what we hoped was my mom's car.

Finally. We were saved.

My mom had several terrible excuses. The truth was she got drunk and fell asleep/forgot about us. We drove home in almost complete silence. She knew she messed up and she felt bad. I was too angry, embarrassed, and tired to even give her a hard time about it.

I was really, really glad when the Cavs moved into Gund Arena downtown 6 years later.

The First Cut is The Deepest

My editor Anna just called and told me that if we wanted to sell more than 12 copies of this thing we were gonna need to spice it up for the housewives. We were gonna have to add at least one chapter about my sordid sex life. The only problem with that is that I am really trying to keep these stories as honest as I can. Since I got together with my wife at such a young age, I really don't have a very exciting sexual history. Certainly nothing to brag about. You could count the number of sexual partners I have had in my life on one hand. Even if you were a butcher missing a digit...

While I lack the excitement you find in romance novels, I more than make up for it in embarrassing true life misadventures. I knew from my very first attempts with the opposite sex that I was no great lover. I was no great fighter either, I have always been more of a sardonic commentator and observer of women. I have found that even though every women's magazine tells you that the number 1 thing women are looking for in a man is a great sense of humor, the truth is that the sense of humor in question had better be attached to a good looking man with a big wallet or a big dick and clearly, I lack all of the above.

The truth is that there really is someone out there for everyone but most people don't find that person in high school the he way I did. This story is not about Megan, it's about the woman who helped me become the irresistible lover that Megan fell in love with.

It was the winter of 1991 and beginning of 1992 when I was picked up by an older woman at a Wendy's in Euclid. She saw the way I was manhandling a classic double cheeseburger and she had to have me. Her name was Linda and she was a 17 year-old junior at Euclid high school. Ian was with me when she asked me for my phone number and he thought she was kind of fat but I thought she was hot! I had always been attracted to bigger girls, even at 15. I'm not Freud but I am sure that I was looking for the polar opposite of my mother, who was short, skinny and had no boobs (unless she was pregnant). I have read that women often subconsciously look for men that remind them of their fathers and maybe since I had such a strong dislike for my mom at that age I did the reverse? Either that or the 400 pre-pubescent viewings of Revenge of the Nerds had secretly made me attracted to the Omega - Moos. Who knows?

But it isn't fat girls that I like- I'm not a chubby chaser- I just like big boobs and I know that those usually come in tandem with big hips and a big butt. I grew up with a lot of black kids so I like hot sauce and soul music too, don't make me feel weird because I have a strong appreciation for the thick girls as well. You skinny broads are probably really nice but you can't do a thing for me! Linda and I went out on a few actual dates and we were getting along ok when during a conversation on the phone she asked me if I was a virgin. I was only 15 so I told her the truth. I was too young to be embarrassed by the fact that I was still a virgin. Most of my friends still were too. I had made out with girls and done some things but I hadn't even attempted to have sex with anyone in real life yet! I had only taken my pants off with a girl once before! So I was kind of shocked when Linda said, "Well, we will have to fix that next weekend!" Who was I to disagree with her plan?

I had a boner that whole week leading up to our date on Friday night. If you grew up in the eighties all you ever saw on TV were commercials telling kids to practice safe sex. It was so ingrained into our generation that we were going to get AIDS that there was no embarrassment left when it came time to buy condoms for yourself. I was proud to buy them, I wanted everyone to know that I found a girl who was gonna have sex with me! I could never understand when I would hear friends talk about how they hated buying condoms. And even at 14 or 15 when I would hear that complaint I would say to myself that you clearly were too immature to be having sex in the first place!

When Friday night came along we went to see a movie at the Lake Shore Theater but we just made out the whole time. After the movie we drove to an empty parking lot at Wildwood State Park on Neff Road and

parked in the back, away from the lights. After we
kissed and made out for a little Linda asked if I wanted
to go into the back seat. Of course I did.

The problem was that Linda was driving her older
brother's car, a 1981 firebird. It had bucket seats in the
back so it really wasn't very conducive to what we were
attempting. I was trying to take things kind of slow to
give Linda a chance to change her mind but she looked at
her watch and asked if I brought protection. She had to be
home at 11 and it was getting late. As I was putting a
condom on myself for the very first time my boner kind
of disappeared and I started to panic. Teenage boys
walk around hiding erections 96% percent of the day
but now when I actually had a use for mine it was
gonna turn on me??? My mind was racing trying to
figure out what I was doing wrong but Linda took her
bra off and my boner came roaring back to life before
she had a chance to say, "What's wrong?"

Next thing I knew I was doing it. For real. Linda told me
that she had done it once before but she seemed like she
was really uncomfortable, either laying on the hard
plastic piece separating the two seats was getting to her or
she was also a virgin.

I remember telling my younger sister once that the first
couple times you have sex it is so terrible that you
might as well just wait until you were with someone you

really cared about. I wish someone would have warned me about this. The few friends of mine who were not virgins had warned me that it would be over so quick that I would be mortified. I started to get worried that I was doing it wrong because we were already moving past one full minute and I had not reached any kind of climax that I was aware of. Linda seemed to get a little more comfortable the longer we went and for a second I thought that maybe I was good at this after all.

That was when I saw the police lights. Cops turned on a flood light aimed at our car and Linda instantly panicked. We both put our clothes on in record time when the officer knocked on the window of the car. Linda was crying. It was not how I pictured losing my virginity at all. The officer took her license and my high school ID because it was all I had. He kind of chuckled and said, "Sorry kids, but the park is closed. You guys have to get out of here. It's late, why don't you get home" as he handed us back our ID's. As we drove away Linda was able to stop crying and we both actually kind of laughed at how ridiculous the whole thing was. I think even the cop was embarrassed. As she pulled into my driveway I realized that I still had the condom on. What an epic failure!

The next day I had to check with Rob Tepley to find out if I was still a virgin or not. Technically I had put my penis into a vagina but I never finished so I was unsure of the ruling. He was an expert, he had already had 2 or possibly 3 sexual partners so we all trusted his judgment on these matters. He assured me that I was no longer a virgin but that I needed to "get back in there and finish the job!"

I called Linda later that week and broke up with her. She was so nice to me but I was so embarrassed about my "performance" that I didn't think I could ever face her again. The whole thing was a mess. Why did I get a softy in the middle of the act? I guess I could blame the condom but I didn't know and I didn't exactly have anyone I could talk to about it. My older brother was away in the Marines, my dad was living in Pittsburgh and I didn't want to write him a letter to tell him that I may be impotent. I couldn't bring myself to talk to Gil about school or sports so I sure as hell couldn't talk to him about it. I just swallowed the whole thing and when I finally had a chance to have sex again at a party two years later, everything worked much better so I just forgot all about the whole episode. I think the truth of the matter was that I was scared. I wasn't ready to have sex yet and my body tried to stop me.

Don't worry about it, ladies. I am much, much better at sex now. You'll probably still go home unsatisfied but I'll do better, I promise.

The Temple of Doom

I have never been a very violent guy, it usually takes quite a while to get me upset, but when I do get upset I go from zero to belligerent in no time at all. I first started to notice this talent when I was nine years old. My older brother Warburton used to keep snakes as pets. He would catch them in the woods or down by the lake. He had a giant wooden cage in the basement where he kept them and the smaller, skinnier snakes would constantly get loose. I wasn't afraid of snakes but I definitely thought they were creepy. When one would escape Warburton would announce to everyone to keep an eye out for a 2 foot long black snake that must have gotten out of the cage last night- like my childhood wasn't scary enough- Now I have to worry about rogue reptiles slithering under my covers while I tried to sleep.

Most of the time my Mom was the lucky one who would find them. She would reach her hand into the dryer looking for a clean pair of pants only to find one of these cold-blooded monsters coiled up around her Calvin's. We would hear a bloodcurdling scream coming from the basement and Warburton would take off running down the stairs. It is probably the reason that Mom stopped doing the laundry altogether soon after! It was psychological terror that my big brother was raging against us. One night while we were eating dinner Warburton comes up from feeding his snakes to

make his familiar announcement that there was a loose
snake somewhere in the house. My sister Bel said to me
"He better hope to God that I don't find that snake,
because if I do, I'll kill it!"

I agreed with her and secretly hoped that she would.

Fast forward a couple of weeks and this snake still
hadn't turned up, but we did find an almost perfect
mold of the snake when he shed his skin in my parents'
bedroom so we knew he was probably still in the house.
I was 9 years old and already dreaming of the day I
could get out of this house of horrors and this dumb-ass
snake manages to escape the cage but stay in the house
somewhere? That's like breaking out of your prison cell
but not leaving the yard! I was on Bel's side, this snake
was a disgrace to snakes everywhere and deserved to
die!

Two days after we found the skin that had been shed I
was in the kitchen minding my own business making
myself some lunch when I reached up into the cupboard
to grab some peanut butter and sure enough that fuckin'
snake dropped right on to my arm! I grabbed the snake,
ran and threw it as hard as I could out the back door. As
it slid across the back of our driveway I went insane.
Ignoring both Morrighan and Bel's screams I ran into
the backyard after the snake I just threw and picked it
up by its tail. My sisters ran towards the house afraid

that I was gonna throw it at them. I took that snake and started spinning it over my head like it was Indiana Jones' bull-whip and screaming my brother's name. Tears poured down my face as I unleashed a barrage of blue language that would have made a sailor blush. I was spinning that snake with Roger Daltrey-like force and speaking in tongues. This was probably my first psychological break from reality.

As Warburton came running up the driveway I screamed "I found your Goddamned snake!" and watched in horror as the snake broke in two because of my spinning. The end with the head went flying over the fence into the McNeil's backyard leaving me holding 4 inches of a dead snake's tail in my hand. Warburton's eyes grew big when he realized that I just murdered his missing snake. He punched me hard in the stomach and I crumpled and tried to catch my breath. I threw the piece of snake I was holding at his back as he ran to go tell my mom. I caught my breath and wiped the tears from my eyes. Bel looked at me with a smile and said "THAT WAS AWESOME!"

Warburton retaliated by taking a shoebox full of Raiders of the Lost Ark and E.T. collectible cards and dumping them in a swimming pool. Those cards would be worth 2.1 million dollars in 2017, but it was worth it!

Film School

When I was 19 years-old I worked at the very last full service gas station in the world. In the scorching heat or pouring rain or bitter cold the same dirt bag old men and clueless single mothers would ask me to check their oil or put air in their tires. And I would begrudgingly do it in hope s of them throwing me an extra dollar on the way out but they almost never did. I would stand at the station and pump gas all day long for minimum wage. It was not great. One day a former grade school teacher of mine who still lived in the neighborhood came through and recognized me. "Hey Lachlan, How old are you now?" She asked.

"Nineteen," I said.

"So you finished up with school and now you are pumping gas? That sounds about right..." And she pulled away laughing.

I was crushed. I felt bad enough about myself already. I didn't need a bitter 7th grade teacher to rub my nose in it. It was not a good time for me.

I worked almost every day. My big plan at the time was to save up enough for a decent car so I could get out of Ohio and go start a new life somewhere else. I didn't have a name for it at the time but I think I was in the grips of a pretty serious depression and I had the worst bout of insomnia ever. I had a routine that was the same every day. I caught the bus to my job at 11 AM, rode it to shore center where I would go into blockbuster and rent 2 movies every day. I slowly worked my way through their entire catalog over the course of a year and a half. This was 1994 and the height of Quentin Tarantino and the early 90's indie movie scene. I would read all the magazine articles where people like Scorsese or Spike Lee would talk about how important all these movies from the 60's and 70's were, so I made a note of the titles and directors that were mentioned and I worked my way through their filmographies. I would steal a pack of cigarettes from the gas station and give them to the manager of the blockbuster in exchange for free rentals. I would clock in at work at noon and close up at 9 that night, then I would grab some dinner at Wendy's and catch the 10 o'clock bus ride home. Once I got home I would take a shower and try to get the smell of gas off my hands then retire to my room where I would watch both movies and then try unsuccessfully to get a few hours of sleep. I did this every day but Sunday for over a year. And I wondered why girls didn't want to date me? I'm getting depressed just writing this!

I came home one winter night to my brother Malcolm pretty upset. My mom had come home drunk and got into a big screaming match with Gil, he took off in a fit of rage and she passed out in the kitchen. After the fight my 9 year-old brother asked Mom if she could make him some dinner so she went into the kitchen, put on some water to boil and then passed out. That was two hours prior. This kind of shit was not uncommon around this time. Bel and Warburton were moved out and Morrighan and Feowyn did their best to find friends' houses to sleep over on weekends. Malcolm spent a lot of nights home alone waiting for me to get home. I felt bad for him all the time and it just made me angrier at my mom.

I re-started boiling some water for his macaroni and cheese and I picked my Mom up and carried her up into her room. I took off her shoes and her jacket and put her on the bed. She was snoring the whole time, she could have slept thru a bomb going off in the living room. I had stopped worrying about how much she drank by this point because it was no use. I just tried to avoid being around her as much as I could.

After my brother ate some dinner and I took a shower I asked him if he wanted to watch a movie with me. We were deep into the Stanley Kubrick section this semester and tonight was a double feature of The Shining and Lolita. I had never seen either one but since Malcolm wasn't a big Peter Sellers fan we went with the Shining.

I don't like scary movies but if they were done by good directors I felt like I had to watch them. I really loved Kubrick and Jack Nicholson so I tried to convince myself that it would not be so bad. Plus, I was trying not to look like such a puss in front of my little brother.

I don't think Malcolm liked scary movies either because every time something creepy happened in the movie he would inch a little closer to me on the bed. By the time the little kid started saying RedRum and doing that thing with his finger Malcolm was sitting on my lap with his arms around me. I kept asking him if he wanted to turn it off and he would say no but then tighten his grip on me. Part of me liked it because it gave me something to focus on as Jack started to lose his mind and scare the shit out of me. At the end of the movie neither of us had let go of each other and when we noticed that it was snowing outside we decided to just stay there under the covers and watch reruns of Martin for a little bit. Malcolm was getting ready to fall asleep and he asked if he could just stay in my bed so he didn't have nightmares. I said sure and turned the light out for him. I was gonna stay up and watch another movie but as soon as it started I ended up falling asleep right next to Malcolm. When I woke up a couple hours later he had his arm around me. I hoped that he wasn't scared anymore. I know that I wasn't.

Never Forget that the Golden State Warriors Blew a 3-1 Lead in the 2016 NBA Finals

It was Father's Day in 2016. I woke up with a different feeling than I had ever felt before. I couldn't quite place it, But I felt like we were gonna win that night. The Cleveland Cavaliers were playing in game 7 of the NBA Finals later that night and it was all I could think about the whole day. I won't lie to you and try to tell you that I am some kind of diehard basketball fan because truthfully I am not. But I am a diehard fan of Cleveland, so I will always root for my home teams. The truth is that basketball and baseball seasons are just too long for me to follow. I fully admit that I only really start to pay attention when the playoffs start, but by the time the Finals came around I was ALL-IN!

Football has always been my favorite sport and I will always be a diehard Cleveland Browns fan, but it has been 30 years since they have had back to back winning seasons. Being a Browns fan is a painful, futile and often boring way of life. An entire generation has grown up in this city without knowing what it is like to rally around a good team and expect to win on Sundays. If you go to a home game in Cleveland the stands are usually full with drunk frat guys wearing opposing teams jerseys and their alcoholic girlfriends who are on their phones all day. Very few of the people who can afford to go to Browns games really care about whether the team wins or loses. The only thing more depressing than watching what the Browns do on the field is talking to someone under the age of 35 who calls themselves a Browns fan. It is so bad that I try not to admit that I am still a fan. I have turned down free tickets to games more often than I care to talk about.

Part of the psyche of being a Cleveland sports fan is wrapped up in heartbreaking last minute losses in big games. If you are my age your entire life has involved watching your favorite team somehow snatch defeat from the jaws of victory time after time. There are phrases and names that you dare not mention in certain circles unless you want to see grown men cry. The Drive, The Fumble, The Shot, Jose Mesa, The Decision, The Move. Books have been written about all of these events. I cried harder in 1987 when Earnest Byner fumbled the football on the goal line in Denver than I did when my mother died. The failures of the Cleveland Browns had as much to do with making me into a cynical adult as anything that happened during my childhood. I just expect to lose in the end.

Which is why Father's Day felt so strange to me. The Cavs were playing the Golden State Warriors who had just set the record for the greatest single season in NBA history. They won 73 out of 82 games that season and now the Cavs had to beat them 4 times in order to become champions. We lost to the Warriors in the Finals the year before but some of our best players were hurt so we told ourselves that if we met up with them again and we were healthy, the outcome would be different. The Warriors won the first two games of the series then we split the second two. No team in NBA history had ever come back to win after being down 3 games to 1, especially against a 73 win team! But the Cavs won game 5. Then they won game 6. It was setting up perfectly for another chapter in the book of Cleveland sports heartbreak so I was doing everything I could to not get my hopes up. I had been down this road before... and yet, that morning I had this feeling like maybe this was our year, like maybe the tides had turned.

When I was in the 4th grade I made a bet with my friend Joe, I bet him 10 dollars that the Browns would win a Super Bowl before the Indians would win the World Series. Neither of us even thought that our basketball team had a snowball's chance in hell of ever winning anything. That bet was made over 30 years ago and we are still waiting for someone to win it. I will be over the moon happy to lose that bet one day and hand over 10 dollars to my oldest friend, and he would be just as happy to lose! So we wait... There has been talk over the years of changing the prize of the bet or adding stipulations but we have resisted and kept the bet the same as it was when we thought 10 dollars was a ton of cash. Joe lives in Austin, Texas now but he flew home so we could watch game 7 together, He always said that if Cleveland should ever win a championship he wanted to be in the city when it happened. The fact that he was in town added to the excitement of the day.

Our friends Jacob and Julie Filarski had invited us over to watch the game at their place. It was a Sunday night so Megan didn't want Declan to be out late so they didn't come with me, which was silly because they ended up going to watch the game with my sister Bel and her girls over at Christine Banc's house anyway. I sort of felt bad that I was ditching them but Meg understood that I needed to watch the game with Joe. Our friends Matt Mulichak, Sarah Kempton and Joe's sister Molly all met up with us along with some of Jacob and Julie's friends so there was a nice sized crowd watching the game with us. I don't really need to have reasons to hate the Golden State Warriors but I do have very valid reasons for my hatred. Their two big stars Steph Curry and Klay Thompson are both spoiled rich kids. Both of them had fathers who played in the NBA, they never had to have jobs growing up, fuck that. Kids that are born with silver spoons will never have my respect, no matter how good they are at anything.

Give me LeBron James all day! Give me a kid who grows up in the projects of Akron with a single mother. Give me a kid who knows what it is like to have a Salvation Army Christmas, a kid who knows how embarrassing it is when your mom gets drunk at a little league game. LeBron James may have hit the genetic lottery and grown into a professional athlete's body but every prison in America is filled with similar kids. LeBron James is the greatest athlete that Cleveland has seen since Jim Brown and before his career is over he will go down as the greatest basketball player of all time.

The game itself was a back and forth affair, both teams keeping it close and each making great plays. There are plenty of places you can read about the actual game, that is not what this is about. During the last two minutes of the game. I was as nervous as I have ever been. I just kept looking at the clock and looking at the score then I would look back at the clock. Kyrie Irving made a 3 pointer and a few seconds after that I started to realize that Golden State was gonna run out of time.....I didn't breathe until the clock hit 00:00. I was in shock. WE DID IT, WE ACTUALLY WON A CHAMPIONSHIP!!!!I started screaming and jumping and hugging everyone in sight. I looked at Joe and started laughing because we were both crying tears of joy! It was so stupid to be wrapped up in a basketball game that much yet, here I was openly crying in a room full of people and I didn't even care! I had waited 40 years, my entire life for a Cleveland team to win something and part of me thought I would never get to see it. I kept waiting for that heartbreaking mistake that had always happened when we were close and it never came! I screamed until my throat hurt and I couldn't stop laughing. Next time you wait 40 years for something, I'm pretty sure you won't know what to do when it happens either.

Joe really wanted to go downtown and be with the crowd of people who had watched the game on giant TV screens they set up by the arena so Joe, Molly and Matt jumped in my car and off we went. Joe and Molly had done a couple of celebratory shots so they were pretty much in the bag already. We drove straight down Lorain Avenue from the Filarski's house at Kamm's Corners. At every single bar we passed there were people jumping up and down outside. On the corner of W.130th and Lorain I saw a little old white lady giving hugs and high fives to a group of 4 Puerto Rican kids. Across the street 2 West Side juggalos were hugging an old black guy. And every person you saw had a big smile plastered across their face! I have lived in Cleveland my whole life and I have never seen anything like it! Joe got out of the car and danced with a couple of toddlers who were hanging out on the corner. I'm not sure if they understood what this drunk white guy was so happy about but seeing it made my night!

By the time we got to Matt's to drop him off because he had to be at work so early. Joe may or may not have been passed out in the back of my car. Since pretty much everyone was trying to get to the arena downtown it was bumper to bumper traffic. Every horn in every car was honking and no one was complaining about it for once. We drove up Detroit and parked near the Happy Dog. Joe and Molly went in to get a drink that they were never even charged for and I stood outside watching a parade of cheering Clevelanders driving down Detroit Avenue. I saw Brian Straw absolutely losing his shit and laughing in the middle of the street.

Brian is a musician and friend who I have known for years. I am not a close friend of his but we get along, as soon as he saw me he ran towards me screaming and jumped into my arms! Brian is normally a quiet, reserved indie rock guy, I never would have guessed he was a basketball fan at all but here we were jumping up and down yelling "CLEEEEEVEELAAAAND!!!!" at 1 am on a Sunday! It was seriously one of the happiest nights of my life! After I delivered Joe and Molly back home I had to drive across town to my house. I took the freeway but I drove slow because listening to drunken fans call a sports talk station at 3 in the morning after their team just ended a 52-year championship drought is some of the most compelling radio of all time! When I went to sleep it was almost 4 am and I had to be at work at 8 but it was worth it.

They announced that there would be a championship parade that Tuesday, Joe was supposed to fly back to Austin early Tuesday afternoon. I texted him on Monday night - Sorry to hear you missed your flight, see you at the parade- There was no way in hell I was gonna miss this. I took the day off of work so I could go. Megan's cousin David had come into town just so he could go to the parade as well. So that morning Megan, Declan, David and I set off for downtown. We met up with our friend Lisa Schafer almost as soon as we got there. I texted Bel and her kids and Joe where we were but it turns out that there were over a million people all crowded around E.9th street.

As far as events go, it was pretty weak. We basically just stood in the same place under the hot sun for 4 or 5 hours waiting for the parade to begin, once it did we realized that we couldn't get close enough to really see anything. Cleveland is a pretty segregated city, there is a strong divide between East and West sides with racial hostility bubbling just under the surface, but the night the Cavs won the title and the day of the parade every race and creed and color came together with smiles on their faces. Being in that crowd of over a million people was the most positive crowd this side of a Fugazi show and a cool thing to experience. Normally, large crowds and baking in the sun are two of my least favorite things to do, but I didn't care, I got to hug my son and kiss my wife and know that I took part in the largest gathering of people in the history of Cleveland and it was awesome!!

Reaganomics in Collinwood

I never understand this reverence most people hold for President Ronald Reagan. Not you conservative jack wads, I get why you worship that senile old man. A lot of Liberals forgot how terrible he was and bought in to the Fox news manufactured view of history. Ronald Reagan's policies had a very obvious and tangible effect on my childhood and seemingly overnight decimated a once proud working class neighborhood. When I was growing up in Collinwood, it seemed like everyone's father worked for either LTV Steel, the Ford-Fisher body plant that was near the border of Cleveland and Euclid or they worked for Conrail like my dad and Uncle Ian. Without a doubt Conrail was the largest employer of Collinwood dads that I knew, it seemed like all of my friends fathers or uncles or grandfathers worked for the railroad. We all had similar stories about not answering your phone on weekends, so your dad wouldn't get called in to work overtime or the big derailment that led to everyone getting big glass jugs of wine before Christmas. They were good paying jobs with strong unions and pension plans. Almost all the kids in the neighborhood went to private schools and had stay at home moms.

Fisher body was the first to go. Around 1981, they closed down this enormous facility and moved all of the jobs to Mexico or China where they could pay employees 15 cents a week or some shit. Understand that I could be wrong about the dates and reasons that Fisher closed, but this isn't really the kind of book where I feel required to do any research. These stories are all being told from memory or neighborhood folklore, *get off my back Colombo*! After Fisher body closed down, they didn't need the trains to ship car parts that they made to other factories and they no longer needed steel to make the parts in the first place.

My dad got laid off in early 1982 with almost everyone's dads and uncles and grandpas. I don't know how much money he was getting from unemployment, but whatever it was I'm sure it wasn't enough to support his wife and 5 young children. My mother got her real estate license and started selling houses in the neighborhood. Business was booming at this time since everyone was out of work families started to move to wherever they could find a job. Places like Mentor and Strongsville became boomtowns because they were full of newer factories and warehouses where guys with only high school diplomas could hopefully find decent work. There were a lot of confused looks on the faces of kids in my class when they opened up their lunchboxes. As more and more moms went back to work, the day to day running of the family fell to our fathers. Fathers who thought nothing of packing meat loaf sandwiches or throwing a couple "juke balls" into a Tupperware and expecting their kids to eat these smelly, weird sandwiches without being made fun of. The local Salvation Army started offering after school and summer day camps because all of a sudden no one's Mom was home when they finished school for the day. An entire generation of kids in my neighborhood became latch key kids when the stress of being out of work contributed to everyone's parents suddenly getting divorced. It wasn't just in Cuyahoga County, These things were happening all across the country but the rust belt was particularly hard hit. The prevailing attitude coming from the White House seemed to be that if you were poor, that was your fault.

My father did whatever work he could find, The problem was that it had to be under the table or he would lose his unemployment, No one had any idea if this lay- off was gonna be temporary or long running and since almost everyone in the neighborhood was in the same boat it was hard to find a suitable job. As long as he was collecting unemployment all of his kids were still covered by the unions hospitalization plan, and that was too valuable to risk losing to become a fry cook or bank teller. My dad was able to hire on to a roofing crew and work off the books most of that summer. Jobs like that are fine but all of a sudden no one eats if the foreman goes on a bender or it rains all week. Roofing put a couple of bucks in your pocket and kept the lights on but it sure didn't offer a whole lot of stability. The more forward thinking people in the neighborhood, like my uncle, Ian took this lay off as a sign of things to come and enrolled in college courses so that he could get into an entirely new line of work. My dad on the other hand used his own expertise and started selling weed.

We didn't know at the time that he had branched out into sales, We knew that he smoked a lot of weed with my mom and that they often had friends come over and all their friends smoked weed with them. It was never hidden from us kids so we didn't know that it was illegal and that not everyone got high. This was in the early 80's when every third commercial was Nancy Reagan or some washed up dinosaur rock star like Ted Nugent telling everyone to just say no to drugs, I agreed with them I just didn't know that marijuana was a drug. I had seen enough after school specials to know that drugs would mess you up and lead to prostitution or punk rock! The only thing I ever saw weed lead you to was the refrigerator. As far as we were concerned the only downside to our parents' drug habit was that my dad was convinced that Gunsmoke was the most exciting show on television and our house always smelled like it had been sprayed by a skunk. I remember going over to a friend's house once and he was super embarrassed by the skunky fumes coming from his parent's bedroom. He nervously said to me "Man, whatever my mom is cooking is stinking up the whole house!" I just laughed and said "Yeah, my mom makes this all the time!"

So we knew he smoked it, and we knew that he grew it because there were special aquarium like boxes with super bright lights in his den. We were under strict instructions to never under any circumstance turn off the lights in his den but since us kids had zero interest in reading the collected works of William Blake or Fyodor Dostoyevsky that lined the bookshelves of the den we had no reason to be in there, plus it stunk like weed in there! No thanks. We started to put together there might be something going on because long haired white kids in Judas Priest T shirts would occasionally knock on the door asking for my dad, it was a big pain in the ass for us because we would have to tell them to hold on while my dad tried to find his pants. Then they would both go upstairs to the den for 5 minutes, the hesher would leave, my dad would take his pants off and try to figure out what he missed on that episode of Kung-Fu. I once asked my brother if Dad was really selling pot and Warburton said "I think just a little, to friends."

"Can't he get in trouble for that?"

"Relax, I don't think he is selling very much. If he was a drug dealer why do we have such a shitty car?"

This logic made perfect sense to me. When I was young I would stress about things that little kids should not worry about. I laid in bed at night worrying about the normal little kid issues like striking out in little league, waking up late for school or my mom having any more kids (please, no) and I would worry about things like my dad getting arrested or Russia dropping a nuclear bomb on Cleveland, I would work myself into such a state that I would get sick and throw up. This wouldn't happen all the time but it happened enough for my Mom to notice it and mention it to a doctor during one of my checkups. Then I would stress out that I was making her worry about me, the truth is I was just kind of a sensitive kid who worried too much. Warburton pointing out that dad would be driving a better car if he was making money selling pot put me at ease and I didn't worry about that ever again. Maybe I should have.

In the spring of 1983 while we were in the kitchen eating dinner Mom and Dad told all of us kids that Dad had been accepted to a law school in North Dakota and that he would have to go away to school at the end of the month. It's funny how things that would end up having an enormous effect on your childhood are sometimes hard to remember when you are writing about them 35 years later. At the time I don't remember what we thought when they told us that dad was going away to law school, but thinking about it now I have a million questions like, *who the fuck goes to law school in North Dakota? What could any law school in North Dakota offer that a law school in Cleveland wouldn't? Are you going to be specializing in land rights of buffalo herds' law? Is going to law school while you already have 5 small children really pragmatic? Are you gonna have to start wearing suits all the time because I never see lawyers on TV wearing flannel shirts? Does this mean that you are not going to get your job at Conrail back?* I don't know if we asked our parents any of those questions. The decision had already been made by them and we were gonna have to deal with it.

When my mom tucked me in that night I remember telling her that I was gonna be really sad to have dad gone for so long. She started crying a little and told me, " We're all gonna be sad, so we will have to take care of each other as best we can". That did not reassure me, all I could picture was Warburton playing king of the mountain and throwing us down a hill come winter. Very early into our summer vacation there was a big family meeting called by my mother. We didn't' normally have family meetings so I remember thinking it was very odd. We were all sitting around the dining room table, which was also odd because we only ever used the dining room for Christmas dinner or birthday parties. I remember thinking that things must be serious because my Grandma MacKinnon and Uncle Ian were there with my mom. My mom said that we were all old enough to know the truth (I was 7). Dad was not enrolled at law school in North Dakota but he was actually in prison. He had gotten busted for selling marijuana and was going to be in jail for up to two years. We were devastated.

Earlier that day My sister Bel had gotten into an argument with our next door neighbor Joey Porter over a heated game of four-square, their arguing led to name calling which led to Joey saying, "Oh yeah, well that's why your dad is in jail!"

"What are you talking about, he is going to school!" Bel offered.

"Yeah, at Jailbird University!" Joey said. Some of the other neighborhood kids laughed and Bel started crying and ran home. When she asked Mom about it, my mom didn't have the heart to lie to her anymore. The story we got at the big family meeting is that when Grandma took us all to the movies in the spring the police had come to take my father away. Apparently, everyone on our street knew about this but us. We never heard one peep about dad getting arrested, never heard about trial dates, never heard about the judge letting him postpone his sentence for a few months because his wife just had a baby, never heard about appeals or lawyers or anything. That's a lot of secrets to keep from 4 inquiring minds but this was pre-Internet, we still thought professional wrestling was legit. I do remember talking to Bel later on and we both were really mad that they kept the whole thing a secret from us. We understood telling Morrighan a fib because she was only 6 but Bel and I were practically grown up!

During the meeting my Uncle Ian told us that anything we would need my dad for we could just walk around the block and ask him for help and grandma told us that she was there for us to help in any way we would need. The truth was that Dad had already been gone for a few months, we missed him terribly but things were actually running pretty smooth. Things change pretty quickly sometimes.

Reaganomics in Collinwood Part 2- Electric Boogaloo
Or Christmas in the Clink

S ummer vacation in 1983 was off to a rousing start. Once mom told us the truth that dad was in jail everyone did their best to not make things harder for her. She had her hands full. Mom was trying to sell houses when she could get a few hours without us kids but there were 4 of us and a baby. The 4 older kids would go to the Salvation Army day camp until 2 or 3 in the afternoon but then we were back at home. There were many days when mom was doing important stuff on the phone and we were forbidden to be in the house. My Aunt Micki would ride her bike around the block every afternoon to see if there was anything that we needed and she would watch Feowyn if my mom had to go show a house or something. Our family really did chip in to try to make things bearable for us kids that summer. My Uncle Tommy took me up to Humphrey's field on weekends to play catch and he taught me how to ride a bike. If anyone popped a chain or got a flat tire you would just walk your bike over to Uncle Ian's so he could fix it. My parents' good friends John and Nick took all 4 of us older kids to Geauga Lake and I snuck on to the Double Loop with John, even though I was a good 2 inches too short and scared out of my mind! These are relatively small things, but they mean the world to a little kid.

We would look forward to Sunday afternoons when Dad would get a chance to call us. Talking to Dad on the phone while he was in jail was weird. I tried to downplay anything good that happened because I didn't want to make him feel bad for missing out on it. I wouldn't want to tell him things were really bad either because he was not in a position to help or make things better. I didn't want to hang up with him feeling shitty. My mom would talk to him first and then hand the phone over to us kids, we couldn't take too much time telling him about our week because he was only allotted so much time for his call. I distinctly recall getting yelled at when I was telling him about that week's episode of the Incredible Hulk and how great it was then the line went dead because his time was up and Morrighan started crying (shocker) because she didn't get a chance to talk to him. I don't remember ever asking him how he was dealing with things. When you are 7 years-old your father is the strongest, smartest, toughest person you know, I wasn't worried about him getting beat up or having to be some cellmate's bitch or anything like that, I was too young to know that was even a thing. Even now as an adult, it is something I never asked him about. We have a good relationship and I'm sure he wouldn't mind talking to me about it, it's just something that I have never had the courage to bring up with him. Once, in my twenties we were watching a movie and he said "You know, prison isn't like that at all." I had no follow up questions and I remember Megan being mad that I didn't say anything else on the subject to him.

Once we found out where he was and then later when we found out that everyone on our street knew, I would start to understand why people treated us the way they did.

For every one of our friends who all of a sudden were not allowed to come play at our house with no explanation, there would be someone who would go out of their way to do something nice for us, but also with no explanation. When my mom sent me around the block to the convenient store to buy a gallon of milk, the owner Betty would tell me to grab a couple pieces of Bazooka Joe for my brothers and sisters "but don't tell your Mom" (also- any candy given to me to share with my siblings between 1980-1990 was eaten by me, usually before I got home). Little league coaches didn't mind giving us rides home after games. Mr. Adams stopped collecting for the newspaper even though we kept receiving it. Mr. DiLiberto turned our gas back on when it got shut off, so we could take hot showers before the weekend. You don't realize at the time but a community looks out for each other. We appreciated the generosity but were always wary of pity. Adults who helped you because they felt bad for you, just made it feel worse. It was easier to say, "no, thanks" to anything that smelled like charity.

My mother did a really good job of hiding how tight things were that summer. We started eating a lot more rice and macaroni and cheese, and everything was usually generic or store brands. My brother Warburton rounded up the troops and together we staged a minor coup when we put all 8 of our feet down and said that we refuse to eat generic cereals. At some point during the summer, I caught my mom refilling a box of Kellogg's fruit loops with one of those enormous bags of generic Frooty Rings. I confronted her like an angry husband and said, "How long has this been going on??!!?" It was probably the most upset that I had been through all of this up to that point. I told all my siblings and we did the best we could to choke down our Crisped Rice or Honey O's but when you have been lied to about breakfast, it never tastes the same....

By the end of the summer we were on welfare. I would cringe if my mom would give me food stamps and ask me to run up to the store for a loaf of bread or something, Even though I know for a fact that a ton of families in the neighborhood were also on welfare, I felt like we were the only ones. I would come up with all kinds of excuses to not go with my mom to the grocery store because I would be endlessly embarrassed when she would break out her WIC coupons or her food stamps. It was always best to just offer to stay home and watch the baby.

In the fall, when we went back to school was the first time we started to see a change in my mother. When I told her that the school shirts from last year did not really fit anymore she burst into tears. She would cry for like 2 minutes, take a deep breath, light a cigarette and say "Ok. We will go get you some new shirts." I couldn't understand the crying, but if I waited it out…she would snap out of it and act like nothing ever happened. I don't know how often she did this around anyone else, but I saw it enough to just stop asking her for things. When we would come home from school it seemed like Mom was at work less and less. I walk into the house and there would be my mom, my Aunt Micki, my mom's friend Tammy and sometimes our old babysitters Debbie and Jackie Bambic from across the street.

They were always nice to us, but they were ALWAYS over! I would come home from a trying day of second grade and I would want to drown my sorrows in generic cereal and watch He-Man but I couldn't because the house would be full of my mom's new gang and each one of them had recently had babies so there could be up to 8 extra people sitting around watching General Hospital! It used to drive me crazy!

Taking out the garbage was my chore and I started to notice a lot more beer cans in the trash. My mom was not much of a beer drinker, but Tammy was. Tammy's husband Billy started hanging around the house with Tammy all the time and sometimes Billy would bring his friend Stan over and together they would sit on our front porch and crush cases of beer during the day. We would come home from school and they would be hammered, Billy used to make a joke to me about how funny it would be if he helped me with my homework while he was drunk. This joke was never funny or amusing and when I told him that since I was already in second grade it would probably be too hard for him even if he wasn't drunk. His buddy Stan said "Boy, I'd beat the shit out of any little punk ass kid who talked to me that way!" Stan and Billy creeped me out. They both threw off a vibe that made all of us kids uncomfortable. I hated that they were hanging at our house. Having a couple of loud, drunk hillbilly/biker guys sitting on your porch was so trashy to me. My family may have been poor, and we may have been loud and weird but we were never white trash, these guys were. And while we're on the subject, has there ever been a more white trash name than Tammy? If you name your daughter Tammy, can you really be surprised when she starts smoking at 11 and wearing cut-offs and tank tops to funerals or job interviews?

I don't know that I ever remember seeing my mom really drunk back then, but we could tell that things were not quite right. There are certain things about this time period that absolutely stick out to me, but then there are other parts that I have blocked or if I remember, those memories are fuzzy at best. I remember finding a small Tupperware container filled with white powder that looked like flour in her nightstand. I hadn't seen Scarface yet, so I don't know if I knew what cocaine was, but I was pretty fucking sure that mom wasn't baking any cupcakes in her bedroom. I have memories of things that in my head seem like maybe they happened in a dream or on some long lost TV show and if I write about them it would make them more real and I'm not interested in any of that.

It was a really rough time for all of us and hindsight being what it is I am willing to sort of give my mother a pass on a lot of things. Here she was a young woman with 5 children and a husband in the joint who was trying to keep things together any way she knew how. It's hard to hold a grudge against her because no matter how bad things were for me at the time things were a whole lot worse for her and dad.

Sometime after Thanksgiving, Mom came home from work with big news! We were gonna go visit my dad in Mansfield. We hadn't seen him in almost eight months at this point so we were all really excited about it. We had been talking amongst ourselves about how we knew this was gonna be a pretty lousy Christmas anyway as far as gifts go. Santa was going to stop at our house but nothing very big or shiny was likely to make its way down our chimney that year. So when we found out that we were gonna get to see our dad on Christmas Eve it gave us something to look forward to.

On the morning of Christmas Eve, we all piled into my mom's station wagon drove around the block to where my Aunt Micki and Uncle Ian were waiting with their 3 kids. Our Grandma and the Mackinnon Clan set off on the most depressing road trip of my eight year old life. Driving from Collinwood to Mansfield Correctional Facility is about a 90 minute drive. It had snowed the night before and the roads were pretty icy, so it took us longer to get there. My memory may be fuzzy, but I am pretty sure we were in the car for a minimum of 17 hours before we finally hit the exit to our destination. We were following my Uncle Ian's car but as we rolled around a bend in the road our station wagon hit a patch

of black ice (the most aggressive kind of ice) and slid
into a ditch. Thankfully no one was hurt as we weren't
going very fast, but we also were not wearing seat belts.
A one year old was not in a car seat because it was the
80' s and instead sitting on a ten year old's lap because-
safety first! My Uncle saw us spin out in his rearview
mirror, so he circled his car back to where we were.
Then he drove to a nearby service station and was able
to get a tow truck to come get us out of the ditch. We
used to call the station wagon "The Boat" because we
would get seasick from rolling around in the way back,
but we found out that day that it was not a sea-worthy
vessel at all. It's first contact with a ditch full of half
frozen water and we had to call for back up.

We got back on the road and all the anticipation I felt for
the two weeks leading up to this day evaporated as soon
as we drove through the prison gate. All of a sudden it
wasn't fun anymore. There were armed guards and
barbed wire and prison bars everywhere you looked. I
knew my dad was in jail, but this was JAIL with a
capital J. We all had to walk through metal detectors
and everyone had to empty out their purses and pockets.
Watching your sweet old grandmother being frisked on
the way to see her son in prison is not something I
recommend, it tends to put a bad taste in your mouth. I
thought it was strange that even the kids had to be patted
down but this was my first visit to a state run facility so I
didn't know all the rules. I can now tell you from
experience that among all of the things that you cannot
bring into a prison to show your dad, your brand new
Return of the Jedi Luke Skywalker action figure (the

cool one where he is wearing all black) is absolutely prohibited and even if you start crying you will have to leave it at the front desk.

We were led down a long hallway and into a large visiting room where my dad was waiting at a long folding table. He looked good. He had lost some weight, but he was still the same guy I remembered. He was really happy to see us and even though I was in a funky mood because my Luke Skywalker was taken away from me we tried to make the best of it! My dad had Christmas gifts for all of us, everyone got little knick-knacks made out of match sticks.

Mine was a small sailboat, but I'm not sure it would have done any better on the water than our station wagon.

After visiting for an hour or so, my mom gave Warburton some money to take all of us kids into a different room where there was vending machines. We all got snacks, while the adults could talk for a little bit. My cousin Ian (Pronounced EEE-AN) and I were playing hide and seek in the bathroom off to the side. We were fascinated by the bathrooms there. We had never seen steel toilets before and it's really not that hard to impress a couple of uncomfortable 7 year old kids on their first jailhouse adventure. Ian's dad Ian (pronounced EYE-AN) came into the bathroom and yelled at us for making too much noise. Jails have a lot of rules I guess. When we got back to the table with my dad, the mood was completely different. Whatever he and my Mom and grandma were talked about while we marveled at those space age toilets made my dad incredibly angry. He did his best to hide it from us, but between his red face and my mom chain-smoking cigarettes and not talking, something had gone down. We started to say our goodbyes, promised dad that we would write more letters to him and tried to get Morrighan to stop crying.

Everyone filed out of the meeting room and loaded back into our cars. Soon after we hit the road everyone in our car was asleep but my mom and I up in the front seat. My mother had not said more than 3 words since we got in the car. I looked over at my mom and I said "Are you ok, Mom?"

Things will be ok, today was a hard one, but it will be ok." She said, but something in her voice told me that it wouldn't. I didn't like seeing my dad in jail and I'm sure he didn't like us seeing him there. It put a pall over Christmas that year and it stuck with me for a long time. When people grow up and have children of their own, there are a lot of instances where you start to realize that your own parents were just people like you, fumbling forward the best they can. It's something that makes you appreciate all they did for you, but when you see your mom crying or if you visit your dad in prison as a 7 year old it shatters that belief that your parents are

super-heroes a whole lot sooner than it should. I stayed
awake with Mom the whole ride home. We didn't say
anything else to each other, I held her hand and we
listened to *Running on Empty* by Jackson Browne. To
this day the song "the Load Out" bums me out for
reasons that have nothing to do terrible late 70's record
production.

Sometime after the New Year my Mother was making
some tea for my sisters when Morrighan reached up to
the stove to grab the kettle and accidentally spilled
boiling hot water down her chest. I didn't see it happen
but I heard the screaming! My sister was hysterical and
my mom wasn't sure what to do, she called my Uncle
Ian and he rushed over in time to see large chunks of
my sister's skin blistering and peeling off. They rushed
her to the hospital where she was admitted for about a
week to treat her 3rd degree burns. Burns are extremely
painful and the treatment for them is slow and
agonizing for people of any age, but absolutely
heartbreaking for a 6-year old girl. My mom stayed by
her side for the two weeks that Morrighan could not go
to school. Warburton cleaned the house, Belphoebe
made dinner and I read Morrighan her copy of
Cinderella while my mom changed the bandages on her
chest and legs and applied all kinds of ointments and
lotion to her skin. When Morrighan went back to
school, we noticed Mom was not going back to work
during the day. Her female street gang started coming
around again and with them Billy and Stan and a lot
more red and white beer cans in the trash. If it was the

movie Goodfellas, it would be when Ray Liotta says, "This was the bad time."

Maybe Morrighan's burn was just one crisis too many for mom but there was a marked difference in the way she acted for the first part of the new year. This was when we started running out of food in the refrigerator and the first times we would see mom drunk. Her and her friends stopped hanging out so much at our house which was great, until we realized that meant they were hanging out at those dirtbag biker bars that littered E.156th St. Mom wasn't home to help with homework and when we ran out of milk, we started giving Feowyn Kool-Aid in her bottles at night. My sister Belphoebe felt so bad years later about doing this, that when Feowyn's teeth started to decay as a teenager that Bel actually paid for Feowyn to get braces.I should remind you that Bel was 9 years old at the time and when there is no milk in the house and a crying 2 year old who needs a bottle you improvise. We started to feel like when we asked Aunt Micki or Grandma for help, what we were also doing was ratting on mom. Everyone knew that she was struggling, but didn't really know how to help and we kids didn't want to make it worse.

For my 8th birthday, Mom told me a secret- Dad was coming home early that summer! Obviously I kept that secret for about 12 minutes before telling everyone! We were so excited to have him back and as soon as summer rolled around and he was home things seemed to get immediately back to normal. Whatever my mom was doing when he was gone seemed to be over, she wasn't selling real estate, but she did get a job working for a gym. After all the hippie burnouts had spent the 70's freebasing cocaine and listening to garbage like Fleetwood Mac. They decided to get healthy in the early 80's, so they cut back on the coke and got gym memberships and started doing Jazzercise. They still listened to garbage music though. Mom stopped going to bars, her gang came over less often and we hardly ever saw Billy or Stan anymore. As much as I want to believe that things were back to normal when my dad came home there were some things that never returned. There were a lot less trips to Euclid Races for ice cream and a lot less going out for dinner but it was great to have dad back in the house. Even if he and mom fought more often.

By the time Ronald Reagan had been reelected in a massive landslide, there were 3 black families on Grovewood and 5 or 6 more For Sale signs. White Flight was in full effect in Collinwood and boarded up factories started to litter the southern half of the neighborhood. Conrail had been bought out and most of the guys who were still working under the table jobs were able to get their jobs back if they were willing to move to Toledo. My dad didn't have a ton of options as his new felony conviction probably would have stood out on his resume, so he took a job working in Toledo. For the next two years or so, he would work 10 hour shifts Thursday thru Sunday and commute back home late Sunday night until he left on Wednesday. It was hard on him and it was hard on us.

Mom wasn't drinking anymore but we never could get used to Dad's schedule and it seemed like he was still not around when we really needed him. In 1986, my younger brother Malcolm was born and Conrail was sold again. My dad was transferred to Pittsburgh and when my mom flat out refused to move to be closer to him it was the final nail in their marriage. My father wanted his family to be with him under one roof so he bought a big house in a Pittsburgh suburb and decided to drive us all out there and show it to us on my Mother's birthday. She was so upset that he never talked about this with her before doing it that she made up her mind before ever seeing the house or neighborhood that she would not be uprooting the family.

I don't know all the details of what was going on between my parents at the time and it isn't my place to say who was right and who was wrong. I thought they both had valid reasons but I was like 10 years old and the only thing I was sure about is that wherever we lived, I would never root for the Pittsburgh Steelers.

That house in Pittsburgh was a last chance. The last chance for my parents to save their marriage, The last chance for us kids to get a normal upbringing, the last chance to be able to sell the house in Collinwood before drug dealers took over the neighborhood, maybe even the last chance for my mother.

Everything changed after they finally got divorced.

The Hit and Roll

O ne of the conditions of my probation from "The Dookie Riot of 1994" was that I had to remain clean for one full year and if I did then the bogus disorderly conduct conviction would be expunged from my record. This was not a problem as I was straight edge already, the problem for me was that I would have to take a weekday off of work and take a bus downtown. I still didn't have a car because earlier that year I made what would turn out to be the soundest financial decision of my life when I sold the pick-up truck with 254,000 miles on it that my dad gave me for free to my mother's boyfriend Gil for 800 dollars so I could go to Heights Guitars and finally afford that bitchin' Gibson SG that I had been dreaming about. I may have rode the RTA everywhere for 2 years, but that guitar has been played all over the world. Let's face it, that guitar is still melting faces today long after that truck was towed to a junkyard somewhere on the east side.

My manager at Fuel Mart, the gas station I worked at would always get mad when I would need these days off because it would usually mean that he would have to stay and pump gas until the stations third employee could get there after school. Even though Sean, the manager would have to deal with a record number of customer complaints about me, he knew he could depend on me to be there Monday-Saturday 12-9, no matter what.

I would look forward to these visits because after I went to the justice center and peed in a cup I would go over to tower city and sneak into a movie or two. I discovered that the security at Tower City early in the day was virtually non-existent, so if you bought a ticket to get into one movie you could just walk into another theater and see a different movie when it finished. It's not like I had anywhere to be so I would grab some lunch and make a whole day of it.

I had to be at my probation officer's desk before eleven am the morning of the 20th of each month. If the 20th was on a weekend then I would have to report on the Monday after. The following incident happened on one of those Monday mornings so it was extra busy because there were 3 times as many parolees waiting to pee in cups.

The morning was off to a rough start as it started pouring down rain almost as soon as I got off the bus downtown. I only had a two-block walk from the bus stop to the justice building but since I have never owned an umbrella, it was long enough for me to get drenched. The probation office was in the basement of the justice building so I had to squeeze my dripping wet ass into a crowded elevator and hit the B button. As soon as I pressed the button, I could feel 12 sets of eyes

looking at me like the hardened criminal that I was.
Frankly, it was embarrassing.

After I checked in at the office, I was told to sit and
wait until they called my name. I don't know if it was
walking in the rain that did it but as soon as I sat down I
had to pee. Bad. 20 or 30 minutes passed and I got up to
explain my situation to the secretary. She told me that I
would have to wait my turn. The first month I had to do
this, I became very pee-shy and it took four trips to the
water fountain before I could fill the cup. I wasn't used
to relieving myself while a large black man with a badge
stood over my shoulder watching and my bladder decided
not to cooperate. Today was the exact opposite situation,
if they didn't call my name in a hurry I was gonna wiz on
the floor in front of 15 other lowlifes!!!

Thankfully, my name was called before I had an accident
and me and my buddy, officer number 1 (get it?) ran to
the bathroom where I proceeded to pee for 12 minutes
straight. The state of Ohio got what they needed from me
and I was free to go.

Got in the line for the elevator to leave when all of a
sudden I was almost knocked over by an electric
wheelchair! I got my balance and turned around
expecting an apology when I see that fat crippled
motherfucking lawyer Jeff Friedman just keep rolling!

"Hey! Watch it, Asshole!" I screamed, but it was no use, this bald piece of shit had one of those early 90's cell phones that were the size of a brick jammed up to his repugnant face. He heard me but this fucking prick just hit the gas on his motor and rode off into the sunset. It was bad enough that the bus I took downtown had an advertisement for Friedman, Domiano and Smith plastered on the side of it. But I guess just looking at his ugly mug while I was losing a day's pay so I could piss in front of a cop wasn't humiliating enough for me, Now I have to deal with a heartless Jabba the hut driving by taking out people's knees while he has phone sex at 11am, Then can't even be bothered to throw me a halfhearted apology!?! This dirty motherfucker shows up on my tv in commercials where he has his pants pulled up to his nipples trying to elicit sympathy because he hasn't been able to get a boner since Jimmy Carter was in office but in real life he is too concerned with trying to get back to his office before all the donuts are gone to pay attention to traffic rules or common decency? No way, I'm not playing your games Mr. Friedman, as far as I'm concerned you still got payback coming! And if you think I'm gonna go easy on you because your spine is broken, you are dead wrong! I pray that I see you flying towards me some day because no matter what I am doing I will launch myself at you and clothesline you right out of that fuckin chair! And that's a promise! Ha ha ha!!

An Oral History of My Summer in Traction

It was actually spring ... In April of 1981, just before my fifth birthday, I was hit by a car. I was crossing the street in front of my house. It was the first of many times in my life when I probably should have been accompanied by an adult, but was not. I suffered pretty serious injuries to the right side of my tiny body, including a broken leg, cracked ribs, a fractured skull, and severe emotional distress. In an effort to clear up several long-running family controversies regarding this incident, I have enlisted the help of Carl Monday. Together we have conducted an independent investigation and multiple interviews with any and all surviving parties. Although memories differ about 35 year old neighborhood tragedies, we hope that this document becomes the definitive account of these events, which will finally clear any consciences and answer all questions. Enjoy!

Warburton MacKinnon (older brother): It was one of the first nice weather Saturdays of the year, so all the kids on the street were outside playing. Most of them were at our house.

Belphoebe MacKinnon (older sister): Warburton was being a total jerk and wouldn't let any of the younger kids join the football game that he and the bigger kids were having.

Warburton MacKinnon: They could have gotten hurt. I was protecting them!

Jeffery Zahoworski (oldest neighbor on scene): I was the official quarterback. It was Warburton and Melvin versus Jeff Linceetar and Michael Frantz. Warburton's team was taking a beating.

Warburton MacKinnon: I wouldn't say we were taking a beating...we were down by onscore!

Melvin (neighborhood stoner; name withheld upon request): Wasn't really a big sports guy anyway.

Jeff Lineceetar (neighborhood kid): I could not be covered!

Lachlan MacKinnon (victim): I was going across the street to Danny Hurtack's house to play. I was carrying my Batmobile. I asked Warburton if it was OK to cross the street, because I wasn't allowed to cross by myself. He said, "GO! Run. You got it!"

Warburton MacKinnon: I said, "NO! Do not go!"

Jeff Lineceetar: I told him, "Run! You got it! Don't dilly dally and take your sweet ass time!"

Warburton MacKinnon: It was fucking third down!

Belphoebe MacKinnon : I yelled for him to wait.

Danny Hurtack (best friend; lived directly across the street): I don't know who yelled what, but Lachlan was not walking quick enough. I just happened to look up from my race cars in time to see him get fucking demolished by a fast moving Buick!

Jeff Lineceetar: Kid got laid the fuck OUT!

Danny Hurtack: That Batmobile did not survive.

Morrighan MacKinnon (younger sister): I screamed at the top of my lungs and started crying.

Jeffery Zahoworski: I heard the brakes screech and someone scream. I looked up and Lachlan was literally in the air! It was scary. We were sure that he was dead.

Warburton MacKinnon: I ran towards the street to see if he was OK.

Belphoebe MacKinnon: I immediately ran into the house to wake up Dad.

Melvin: I ran home. I did not want to get blamed for this!

Jeffery Zahoworski: Lachlan was laying, motion less , in the street. He was bleeding pretty hard from his head. He was unconscious, but breathing. I put my tee shirt against his head to try and stop the bleeding. I knew that it was very important to not move someone who had been injured. Mr. MacKinnon was running out of the house. In his underwear.

Jeff Lineceetar: I was like eleven! When I got nervous, I would kind of giggle. I was really nervous; I just saw my friend's little brother get killed. When I saw his dad run out of the house in boxer shorts, yeah... I started laughing. But it was more because I was scared than because it was funny.

Ivan Yurkovic (borderline racist and totally made up name of the driver of the Buick): I never see kid. My car big and that kid was very short. I never even see him.

Jeffery Zahoworski: As Mr. MacKinnon was running towards us, the fucking car beeped his horn for us to move!!!

Jeff Lineceetar: Yeah. I lost it when the guy beeped at us.

Ivan Yurkovic: The beep was accident. I was scared and running late for work.

Bill MacKinnon (father): I was still half as lee p when I saw him in the street. I never heard the beep.

Leslie Hurtack (Danny's mother; neighbor): I called 911 as soon as I realized what had happened. ran outside and told Bill that an ambulance was on the way.

Belphoebe MacKinnon: Dad told me to run inside and get his pants and shoes.

Bill MacKinnon: I wasn't about to wait for an ambulance in our neighborhood, so I scooped Lachlan up in my arms and put him in the backseat of the car. We tore off for the hospital.

Jeffery Zahoworski: I told Mr. MacKinnon that he shouldn't move an injured person, but he didn't listen.

Warburton MacKinnon: As Dad was putting on his pants, he told me to not let the driver leave until the cops came. He told Bel to go in the house and call Mom at work. Tell her to meet him at Rainbow. Then, call Aunt Micki and ask her to come over here.

Belphoebe MacKinnon: Mom went crazy on the phone when I told her what happened.

Warburton MacKinnon: The ambulance got there about five minutes after Dad left. A Police car showed up right behind them. The EMTs told us that you should never move an injured person.

Belphoebe MacKinnon: Aunt Micki ran through the Danko's backyard and got to our place before the ambulance.

Micki MacKinnon (aunt): Bill had already left when I got over there. I just tried to get Morrighan to stop crying. I was trying to find out what happened when the police arrived.

Warburton MacKinnon: Both Aunt Micki and the cops were asking me who was supposed to be watching Lachlan. It felt like they were trying to blame me.

Jeff Lineceetar: I took off when I heard sirens.

Jeffery Zahoworski: The cops kept asking if I knew how fast Mr. Yurkovic was driving, but I couldn't tell. It didn't seem like he was flying down the street or anything. I kept telling them that I was playing football and not paying attention to the traffic. We all had to give them our statements and tell them our parents' names and phone numbers. Kinda felt like we were all in trouble. I didn't like it at all.

Ian MacKinnon (cousin): My sister, Gwen, and I walked around the block later that day when we heard what happened. There was a big bloodstain in the middle of Grovewood Avenue.

Lachlan MacKinnon: I don't have many memories of any of this, but I distinctly recall waking up in the backseat of Dad's car. Even then, I thought he was driving like a wild man!

Bill MacKinnon: I made it from Collinwood to Rainbow Babies & Children's Hospital in about nine minutes. That is exceptional for a Saturday. I ran four red lights, but figured that the dying kid in the backseat would be good for getting me out of a ticket if I got pulled over. He woke up for a couple of minutes while I was speeding down MLK Boulevard, and started crying. I took that as a good sign, actually. By the time I got to the hospital, he was passed out again. I picked up Lachlan and ran into the emergency room, where the doctors took him and got to work. While the doctors were working on Lachlan, I called home and spoke to Warburton, to make sure that everyone was ok.

Warburton MacKinnon: Dad called and he was pretty pissed. He didn't say anything, but it felt like he was blaming me for the whole thing... which was total bullshit!

Bill MacKinnon: My wife Laure, showed up just before the doctor came out to give us an update. Lachlan's worst injury was that his leg was broken in several places. They were going to take him to surgery to install a rod just below his hip. That would run down to his knee, where they would install three screws to keep everything in place. He had a fractured skull and probable concussion, but the doctor wasn't too worried about that. The doctor also explained that Lachlan was going to need a cast around his waist to protect his two broke n ribs. The good news for us was that although he had serious injuries, he would ultimately be fine. Then he told me that I should never move an injured person. Laure rolled her eyes at me.

I didn't need her fuckin' attitude!

Belphoebe MacKinnon: Mom and Dad didn't get home until really late, but they told us that Lachlan had a broken leg. He was alive and he was gonna be ok. They said that if we were good, we could go visit him in the morning.

Lachlan MacKinnon: I woke up in some god damned Craftmatic Adjustable Bed, in a freaking body cast! My head was all bandaged up and the cast ran from my foot to my nipples! My leg was being held up in the air from wires, so I was stuck flat on my back. I couldn't find any way to get comfortable. I had to pee into a plastic bottle, and there were like five other broken kids in the room with me.

Ian MacKinnon: Lachlan was gonna be in the hospital for three to four weeks. He'd be in traction while his leg was set in place. Doctors said that even after they let him go home, he'd remain in the cast for an additional ten to twelve weeks. He was in a *FOUL* mood for almost his entire stay at the hospital. He was just miserable.

Lachlan MacKinnon: Oh, ya think???? You try lying in bed, in the exact same position for a month, while everyone you have ever known comes to gawk at you! Pointing at the cripple! It's not fun! Every night, Mom would tell me that she would be here "first thing in the morning." But when I would wake up at 7am, there would be no one here but a Puerto Rican nurse, named Nancy, to hand me a fresh pee bottle! It would sometimes be almost 10 o' clock before Mom got here. Even then, she would have some bullshit story about needing to go to work, or some other excuse to get out of here as fast as she could.

Warburton MacKinnon: When we would go visit him, Lachlan was so mean to everyone. I know he was in pain, but he really tore into people. Our grandparents came to visit him on his 5th birthday. They bought him a stuffed toy of the Muppets and Lachlan said, "Gee, thanks." Then he whipped it right at Grandpa MacKinnon's head! It got to the point where we didn't want to visit him at all.

Lachlan MacKinnon: First of all, no one in the history of kids had ever chosen Scooter as their favorite Muppet! I'm stuck celebrating my birthday in a hospital bed and they show up with a bootleg gift like that? You'd be upset, too!

Belphoebe MacKinnon: Worst. Party. Ever.

Lachlan MacKinnon: I probably could have handled things a little bit better. I am sorry for hitting my grandfather with a Muppet, but you have to understand the kind of shit I was going through!

Ian MacKinnon: The nurses put together a little party for all the sick kids on that floor for Easter. They even brought in a bunny rabbit for the kids to feed and pet. Lachlan wasn't really into that, either. It just killed him to be stuck in that bed, the way he was.

Lachlan Mackinnon: Yeah, thanks, but no thanks, Nancy! Do you know how many Easter eggs a kid in traction was able to find that morning? How about none. Unless you hid one in my fucking bedpan, there was almost no chance of me finding it.

Belphoebe MacKinnon: We went to see him on Easter Sunday. While he was yelling at Mom, Morrighan accidentally stood on the weights that were holding his leg in place. He started SCREAMING.

Morrighan MacKinnon: I didn't know! It was an accident.

Lachlan MacKinnon: Accident, my ass! That was attempted murder! I don't care that she was only 3 years old; she knew what she was doing. Everybody is all dressed up in their Easter best, and on their way to eat delicious pork chops at Grandma's, but Morrighan isn't getting enough attention so she decides to add 40 pounds of pressure to the weight that is holding my fragile, little bones in place. You're goddamned right I screamed!

Bill MacKinnon: It was a welcome relief when he was released from the hospital. He was still in a body cast, but he could get a round with crutches. His mood got much better.

Morrighan MacKinnon: No, it didn't.

Megan Mullally: I don't really remember Lachlan in nursery school, but I do remember when Mrs. Cavanaugh told us that he got hit by a car. He wouldn't be coming back to school that year. Everyone in the whole class made him get well cards.

Lachlan MacKinnon: I threw those cards in the first dumpster that I could find. Bunch of garbage if you ask me!

Warburton MacKinnon: We all felt kind of bad that he was stuck in that cast, but it was summer by this point. There were only so many games of checkers or Candyland that you can really handle.

Lachlan MacKinnon: My friends were pretty cool about coming over to see me, once I got home. I was still stuck in that body cast, so I was kind of confined to the porch.

Brian Johnson (neighborhood friend): I invited him to my fifth birthday party. I think he felt weird about his cast.

Lachlan MacKinnon: Do you know how hard it is to break a piñata when you are in a fucking body cast??? Well, let me tell you... it's pretty fucking impossible! It's even more impossible to scramble for any of the candy when some able bodied 5 year-old manages to break it open because you no longer have the ability to bend over! The whole summer was a goddamn Shakespearean tragedy!

Bill MacKinnon: Mr. Yurkovic had been cited by the police for reckless operation of a motor vehicle. We were sitting on a mountain of medical bills, so I talked to a friend of mine, named Jack, who had recently passed the bar exam. He told me that this was an open and shut case, and that if we sued him, that we were sure to win. He even offered to do it pro bono. We had nothing to lose.

Lachlan MacKinnon: I was just a kid, but I probably should have been suspicious when our lawyer and my dad would hold discussions about our case while sharing a joint. I had a very different opinion of what open and shut meant.

Bill MacKinnon: Jack was new to the game, but I had complete faith in him. We weren't looking to get rich or put this guy in jail. Jack thought that the guy would likely settle.

Lachlan MacKinnon: He didn't settle. My dad told us that we would be going to a trial. Jack gave me very strict instructions not to talk during the trial. He said that my job was to sit there and look cute for the jury. I was pretty excited to be missing a week of school. First grade was kind of a drag.

Bill MacKinnon: Listen. I'd rather not talk a whole lot about the trial. Just between us, I have never had very good luck in courtrooms.

Lachlan MacKinnon: My mom made me wear a suit and told me to color. It was so boring.

Bill MacKinnon: We knew right off the bat that Jack was in over his head.

Editor's note: Every attempt was made to contact Jack the lawyer, but Lachlan couldn't remember his last name and he didn't return our calls.

Bill MacKinnon: I don't know how many Nazis that Mr. Yurkovic protected back in World War II, but someone from the old country owed him a big ass favor and hooked him up with a world class defense attorney.

Ivan Yurkovic: I feel terrible for child. I never want to go to court. My wife no let me settle. She get her brother-in-law to be our lawyer. He makes a big deal out of everything.

Bill MacKinnon: The police said that he was guilty. Mr. Yurkovic admitted that he was guilty. This slimy, fuckin' Atticus Finch decides to put the entire system on trial! I kept telling Jack to put a stop to this and object to everything. He just let Gregory Peck go on and on and on! The whole thing was bullshit.

Lachlan MacKinnon: I feel bad about it, but just don't have a whole lot of memories about the trial. I remember my dad saying, "bullshit" a lot, and being kind of pissed. I remember that it seemed like everyone was smoking the whole time. The biggest highlights of the whole week were when my Mom would take me for walks around downtown. I thought that was pretty cool; plus she let me get a hot dog from the cart outside the courthouse. I don't remember much from inside the courthouse.

Bill MacKinnon: In the end, we walked away with nothing because Jack Q. Lawyer was the only fucking guy in town who couldn't prove that Ivan Yurkovic had one too many Slivos with lunch, got behind the wheel of that shitbox Buick, and decided to turn my son into a goddamn pavement pizza. Fuck that guy. I probably am still paying hospital bills for this garbage. Oh, and don't think that Laure didn't try to hold this against me, too. Shit. Jack is partly responsible for my fourth divorce. I really got hosed on *that* one!!!

Lachlan MacKinnon: I recovered fully from my physical injuries and would like to think that the mental anguish, from which I suffer, will subside one clay soon.

Happy Birthday to Me

April 25th 1986, 31 years ago this morning. It was my 10th birthday and I stayed home from school to celebrate. My dad had promised to take me to see a movie or something that day, just the two of us. When you grow up in a big family you really don't get any time alone with your parents and you NEVER get to do things by yourself, so this was gonna be a big deal! I must have pulled some kind of middle child Bullshit to get him to agree to it in the first place. That morning as my brother and sisters gave me dirty looks while they were leaving for school, I had convinced my Morn to make me a special breakfast for my birthday. This was also a pretty big deal as she did not normally make us breakfast- we were a cereal family- but I had pulled that charming, cute, irresistible shit that still works for me in certain situations. So there she was standing at the stove making me Mickey Mouse pancakes because I was now a big 10 year old grown up little boy!

"Lachlan, go upstairs and wake up your father."

"Why? What's wrong, he doesn't like pancakes?" I asked her. She put out her cigarette and calmly said "My water just broke, I am going into labor."

Now, I realize that she had been through this before and she was a tough broad but there was absolutely no change in her mood at all!! No running around, no slap stick movie worrying, nothing?? She just finished making my breakfast and made a phone call?? In her defense, she was still on her first cup of coffee but, I was led to believe that labor pains could wake a lady up??

By the time I had finished my birthday breakfast my Mom had changed her clothes and put makeup on and was waiting by the door for my dad. My dad pulled me aside and said "Listen, I hate to ruin your birthday but Morn is gonna have this baby so we are gonna have to re-schedule our movie day. I'm real sorry.... Oh, you are gonna have to stay here and watch your sister Feowyn today. Aunt Micki will come by later and check in on you guys. I'll call when I can." I was pissed.

(My sister Bel later told me that she just happened to be at recess at St. Jerome's when she saw Mom and Dad drive by on their way to the hospital. They were getting high.) A couple hours later Feowyn and I were marching down the stairs at home playing with plastic music instruments. She was beating on a drum and I was behind her making my jazz debut with a tiny toy saxophone, not exactly the Miles quintet but I felt like we had potential.

My Aunt Micki showed up at the bottom of the stairs with a million questions. "What are you doing?"

"Having a parade" duh, like she never saw a marching band before??

"Where is your Mom? And why aren't you at school?

"Uhh, it's my birthday!" (I never went to school on my birthday. Everyone knows that. Just like I'm not at work right now!)

"Mom is having a baby so they went to the doctor" I explained to her. I then guilted her into making some PB and J sandwiches for Feowyn and I before she left. I was on a roll!Soon after she took off our phone rang. It was my dad calling to tell me that my Mom had given birth to a healthy, happy 9lb baby boy that they named Malcolm. I was kind of bummed that I was gonna have to share my birthday but I was really glad that it was a boy. I was excited to have a little brother!

I got to break the news about our new sibling to Bel, Morrighan, and Warburton as each of them came home from school that day. Around dinner time my dad showed up with Pizza's and an ice cream cake for me. It wasn't the party I wanted but it wasn't so bad.

Happy Birthday Malcolm! Maybe someone send it to his bunker

The Breaks

The amount of injuries I had as a child was enough to drive any parent insane, and since my mom sort of lived on that edge of sanity anyway it didn't take much to push her over. You would think that I never drank a glass of milk in my entire life with the way my bones would break, but we were on WIC, milk was one of the few things that was always in the fridge! I guess I was just unlucky. At the end of our street there was a big empty field that was the perfect size for our games of football, it even had a row of trees along the back fence that were spaced almost exactly 10 yards apart so they served as our built in yard-markers. Most evenings after school all the kids in the neighborhood could be found in this empty lot getting their game on until you heard your parents calling you from down the block or the streetlights came on. On this particular spring afternoon in the year of 1987, our football game was winding down when we heard that familiar parental scream calling our names, My Mom or Dad screaming these weird Gaelic names at the top of their lungs became our version of the Grovewood Bat-signal. Surely, the neighbors enjoyed it as well. ·

Everybody hopped on their bikes and took off down the street, for whatever reason, I didn't have my bike with me that day, and the 45 seconds it would have taken me to walk home was too long to keep my mom waiting, so

I hopped up on my brother's friend Melvin's
handlebars. We had all been warned at various times
not to ride on or let other kids ride on the handle bars of
a bicycle because it was too "dangerous". These were
the same parents who never once invested in a car seat
or bike helmet or swimming lessons for us. The same
parents who chain smoked throughout pregnancies and
simply cut off the moldy part of a block of cheese or
loaf of bread and served us the rest for lunch, so you
can understand why we didn't exactly heed their
warnings the way we should have. As soon as I was up
on those 10 speed handle bars Melvin started pedaling
his ass off, all of a sudden he is Lance Armstrong with
both testicles and we are flying down the side walk. As
we got to my house Melvin rode up the hill in my front
yard and then slammed on his brakes, sending all 60 lbs
of my malnourished body sailing through the air. I
landed awkwardly on one leg and executed a totally
ineffective tuck and roll. I heard a really distinct
cracking sound as I tumbled to a stop near the porch.
Melvin and Warburton obviously thought this was the
funniest thing they had ever seen. Melvin was laughing
so hard he had a hard time steering his bike as he rolled
back down the street to his house. I sat up on the ground
and knew something was wrong, I was crying my eyes
out because my shoulder and arm were on fire!

I had been through this routine before and you definitely
did not want to tell Mom about it unless you needed to
go to the hospital. She was too busy to worry about
non-emergency medical treatment. Once I calmed down
I went in the house and put some ice on my shoulder but

the pain wasn't going away. I knew something was wrong because I could not pick my arm up past my ribs and I had no strength at all in my hand. I quickly diagnosed this as a broken shoulder and decided to bite the bullet and go tell my Mom.

"What the fuck are you talking about? You can't break your shoulder, that's not a thing!" My Mom yelled at me. "Well, something is wrong with it" I offered and showed her how little I could move it. I realize that I wasn't Doogie Howser but I had lived in my body for 11 years at this point and I knew that my right arm wasn't supposed to just dangle off my body the way it was. The real problem was timing. It was Sunday night and anyone who grew up with brothers and sisters knew that Sunday nights during the school year suck. They are very hectic because usually right after dinner someone would realize that they didn't have any clean uniform shirts for the next day or someone would remember about that project you were given six weeks ago that was due in 10 hours. I'm 41 and I still get stressed out on Sunday nights. My shoulder was throbbing by this point. I tried to convince my Mother that I was not faking and that something was seriously amiss. She was pissed now. When my Mom was really angry she would bite down on the inside of her bottom lip and I swear the entire shape of her face would change. She put out a cigarette and grabbed me the good shoulder. She made me take my shirt off and come up to the bathroom so she could get a better look at it. The tears started up again once I tried to lift my arm to get my t-shirt off but when we were in the bathroom looking at it there didn't seem to be anything jumping out at us. My injured shoulder was all purple and bruised but it wasn't very swollen at all. Mom told me that it was just a deep bruise and that it would probably be better in a day or two. She told me to take a shower and put more ice on it.

I couldn't get any sleep that night so I got out of bed early that morning and went to talk to my Mom. I told her that I still couldn't move my arm or pick anything up with my right hand. My sisters felt bad for me because they realized that I was in a ton of pain still and no 11 year old is gonna fake an injury for a second day in a row. My Mom was in the kitchen pouring a cup of coffee and holding my baby brother Malcolm, I went and told her that I didn't think I could go to school that day and that I needed to go to the hospital. She went ballistic.

"There it is, the truth comes out! What is it? Do you have detention today? A test? I am sick and tired of you pulling this kind of shit every time you don't want to go to school, Lachlan!"

I could feel the tears coming, I just said "I can't move my arm?!?" She didn't care. She walked over to the calendar on the fridge and I will never forget the way she said this, "Look , you have a doctor's appointment for baseball on Thursday. If your arm is broken, it will still be broken on Thursday. Now go get dressed, you're going to school!!"

I was so pissed. I couldn't believe that she thought I was faking this, I get it, I was always trying to pull shit to get out of school but this was different, I couldn't move my arm at all! The whole right side of my chest was covered in a gruesome bruise! As bad as my shoulder hurt, having my Mom not believe me was almost more painful. I hooked my thumb through the belt loop of my pants to help support my arm and I walked to school. As long as I was sitting in my desk and could rest my elbow on the front of the desk, the pain was mostly bearable but as soon as I would stand up I would get shooting pains all through my arm.

When I got home that afternoon my Mom asked how my arm was holding up and I just spit out, "What do you care?" and went right up to my room. She let out a chuckle and said "Ohhh so dramatic." I had pretty much made up in my mind that I was never going to speak to her again. I skipped dinner that night, but Bel brought me up a peanut butter and jelly sandwich and a couple of aspirin before bed. It had now become a battle of wills between my Mother and me, I had no choice but to gut it out until Thursday afternoon.

It was the longest week ever. When Thursday afternoon rolled around Mom picked me up from school and she had gone to McDonalds and got me a snack. I ate my hamburger in almost complete silence as we drove to my doctor's appointment. That summer I was moving up a division in little league and you had to get a new physical before you could. This appointment was made months ago and it couldn't have come at a better time. When we checked in the nurses took my height, weight, and blood pressure and told me to have a seat and wait for the doctor. My mom stood off in the corner of the exam room with her arms folded. After the doctor came in and looked at my eyes and ears and checked my reflexes he sat down with my chart and said, "Everything looks normal, is there anything else that I should know about?"

"Well, I fell off of my friend's bike this weekend and I haven't been able to move my arm since."

The doctor helped me take off my shirt and show him how far I could lift my arm. He looked directly at my mother and asked "Did you know that your son has a broken collarbone?" Mom immediately burst into tears, I said "See, I told you!" and I started crying. The doctor said that I would need to get an x-ray and he stepped out of the room. My mom started apologizing profusely to me but I was more upset than ever. The doctor and two nurses stepped back into the room and one of the nurses told my mother to come with her. As soon as the door shut the doctor rolled his stool over to me and got very serious.

"Lachlan, is there anything else going on at home that you want to tell us?" I remember thinking where do I start? But the doctor continued "Did you tell your Mom about this injury as soon as it happened?"

"Yes," I said.

"And she refused to take you to the doctor?"

"YES!"

"Did you show her this bruise?"

"Of course I did, she didn't care!" I told them. The doctor moved his stool a little closer and asked.

"Does your Mom ever hit you? You can tell us, you won't get in trouble." Something clicked and I realized that they were asking me if I was abused and as mad as I was at my Mom I told them that they had it all wrong. I told them that she put ice on it the day it happened and looked at the bruises but that she thought I was trying to get out of going to school or something. I told them how my dad works in Toledo most of the week and that there are 6 of us kids, I told them that she said "if my arm was broken on Sunday that it would still be broken today."

The doctor and the nurse were talking quietly to each other and I started to feel like I was gonna be in trouble for this whole thing. Then I worried that I just got my Mom in trouble. The doctor said to me "Do you want your Mom to come down to x-ray with you?"

"Yes, Please!" I said and I was relieved when they let her back into the room. She was still crying and apologizing. Seeing how upset she was made all the anger I had built up that week melt away. I could see that she felt terrible about it and I actually kind of felt bad for her. She was beating herself up enough for the both of us. My 11 year-old brain was already thinking of ways I could use her guilt about this to my own advantage.

After looking at the X-rays the doctor explained that my collarbone had already started to set the way it was broken and that there was not a lot that they could do at this point unless we wanted to re-break the bone and re-set it.

Thankfully, they advised us against doing that because it sounded painful to me. They gave me this weird brace that I had to wear underneath my shirt for 2 months and I had to put my arm in a sling for 2 weeks but I didn't need a cast or anything. The doctor told me that I was "a tough little S.O.B" and that I had already gone through the worst of it. He said that as it healed my shoulder would get its strength and motion back and I would be ready to go when baseball season started. I remember being embarrassed because I had to ask my Mom what an S.O.B was on the car ride home.

I never had any trouble with my shoulder afterwards but if I acted like it was hurting after a baseball practice I could usually count on Mom offering to buy me some ice cream or something. She never did fully forgive herself and I kept that one in my back pocket and tried to save it for emergencies. If you are one of the hundreds of lucky women who ever get to see me with my shirt off, try not to ask about the weird divot under my neck or why my collarbone sticks up the way it does. It just brings up too many painful memories for me...

Date Night

My first date with Megan was kind of a bust because I asked her to go out while she was at work and one of her co-workers invited herself along. The 3 of us went to see the movie Singles because our love blossomed in a time of grunge. 1992 was a weird time in the world, Bands that I liked were being played on the radio, old flannel shirts were stylish, and all of a sudden I had a girlfriend! Clearly, this time was unsustainable. Since our first date had not gone as planned I convinced Megan to go out with me again the next weekend (without any third wheels). That Friday had gotten off to a rough start as I had failed my driving test when my Mom no-showed and I had to take the test in my giant pick-up truck. I briefly thought about cancelling my date but it was kind of a pain in the ass to get a Friday night off of work and I didn't want to waste it. What could go wrong, right??

I picked Megan up and met her Mother for the first time. Barb loved me, because I was super charming but she didn't understand why I parked 4 houses away on her street. I was embarrassed about my truck so I never wanted to park it in anyone's driveway. I don't know why I wasn't more proud to to drive a giant powder blue Dodge with gold racing stripes that cost me exactly zero dollars, but I wasn't.... We'll just chalk it up to teenage angst or something. Barb told Megan to be home by 11 then looked me in the eye and said "Don't have sex with my daughter!" As if that was an option? And we were off on our second date!

I tried to reassure a thoroughly embarrassed Megan that her Mom was fine, " Trust me, if you ever meet MY mom you'll wish that all she said was don't have sex!!!" I was desperately trying to make Meg laugh because I could already feel date number 2 slipping away...

Then I saw the flashing lights and heard the sirens...I guess I should have been paying more attention to driving than on trying to get a laugh because as I was zooming thru my A list material, I also zoomed thru that stop sign on Grand Avenue. I was really calm as I pulled the car over, I turned to Megan and said "You might have to walk home from here because 1 am probably going to jail..."

Horrible dates 2. Lachlan 0.

"License and registration, sir" the officer said. I handed him the registration and my temporary permit and prayed for a miracle.

"Can I see your license Miss?" The officer said to Megan.

"Umm, I don't have one." she said.

The cop looked at me like I was a hardened criminal and said, "You know you're not allowed to drive without a licensed driver accompanying you.... And who is Frank Anderson?"

"Oh, Uhh... That's my dad."

"Your Dad has a different last name??"

"Uhh, sorry. Stepdad."

"Mr. MacKinnon, please step out of the vehicle" are not words that you hope to hear on your second date.

As I sat in the back of the cop car trying desperately to pull shit out of my ass that would explain why my truck was registered to a stepdad who didn't exist but gave me permission to drive even though I didn't have a license. I also had to do this quickly and in a way that would not implicate my real father, who gave me this truck, in anything. It was, as they say a pickle.

I told the officer the truth about failing my driving test earlier that afternoon and I told him that I hadn't had a chance to switch the registration and put it in my name yet because I was going to do that when I got my drivers license. I just kept talking and throwing more information (lies) at the cop hoping that something would stick! I told him that I really liked the girl I was with and that if they needed to take me to jail and tow my truck, can we at least take her home so she doesn't have to walk in the dark from here.

Finally, the cop had heard enough. He turned to look at me "Kid, shut up."

He stepped out of the car and walked back to my truck to talk to Megan. I watched from the back of a police cruiser and thought how could this day get any worse? I hoped that Megan would save herself, I didn't really care about going to jail but I didn't want to get her in any trouble, too. I was pretty positive that this was our last date and that I would be going to juvie.

The policeman got back in the car and didn't answer when I asked if everything was ok? He finished writing out a ticket and then opened the door for me.

"I'm not gonna tow your car. I want you to get back in it and take your friend home. You don't have a license so you are not allowed to drive so take your ass home now!!!" He said in that shitty, cop tone "Don't let me catch you driving anywhere tonight! You'll have to explain to the judge why you are driving illegally and why your car is registered to someone in West Virginia!! You probably will get a hefty fine and now you won't be able to get a license until your 18th birthday, but I just want you off of the street tonight, Do you understand!!!"

"Yes Sir, Thank you Sir, Thank you."

I took my ticket and got back into my truck and waited for the cop to drive off. I couldn't believe that I was not going to jail.

"Hey Megan, I'm really sorry but I think the only reason that the cop isn't taking me in is so I can take you home."

She completely under stood. She asked me if I wanted to hang out at her house for a little bit but I felt like I had just dodged a major bullet and I told her that I had to just go home. I was gonna have to figure out a way to tell my freaking mother that she was going to have to accompany me to juvenile court on Tuesday and she was not gonna be happy about it.

I walked Megan to her door and apologized for another horrible date.

In true MacKinnon fashion I bought myself 23 dollars' worth of McDonald's garbage and went home to drown my sorrows.

To this day both Megan and I come to a full and complete stop on Grand Blvd.

Opening Day

When you live in the ghetto, Opening Day is not the first baseball game of the season but rather the first nice weather weekend in the spring. The winter in Cleveland usually lasts a minimum of 10 months so when that first 70 degree Friday rolls around, people get a little excited.

Megan and I were living in the upstairs of a duplex on School Avenue in south Collinwood. The family that lived in the house right next to us were two sisters who between them had at least 30 children, all under the age of 10. It was some kind of medical miracle situation over there, children were born in packs or litters. I'm not trying to be crude about this but I have been in schools that had less students than kids in that house at any given time.

On a nice summer day the two sisters and 26 of their kids would set up a grill on their front porch and crank up the slow jamz on the boom box. We never got a positive ID on which kid was named "Squirrel" but he was obviously a disciplinary problem judging by how often we would hear his mother yell "SQUIRREL" at the top of her lungs. Who names a kid squirrel in the first place??

Megan and I both had really stressful days at work that Friday, As we watched the 11 o'clock news and heard them saying that "Tomorrow was gonna be 73 degrees and sunny" Meg turned to me with tears welling up in her eyes and said, "I don't know if I can handle opening day with these neighbors!! I tried to calm her down the best way I could. As we went to sleep that night I prayed for rain. In the morning the delicious aroma of Newports and fresh charcoal wafted through our windows as I told Meg, "Take a shower, let's get out of town."

We got in the car and looked both ways making sure no Squirrels were running past our driveway. We got on the freeway and headed east.

"So, where are we going?" Megan asked.

"Not sure, but we'll know when we see it."

When Megan stopped rolling her eyes we started thinking of where we could go or what we could do. It was a really beautiful day, we had a full tank of gas, a couple of bucks and The Velvet Underground on cassette. It was nice to be on the road. Using the green highway signs as markers we still had not settled on a destination until we started seeing signs for Buffalo. I hated Jim Kelly so I didn't care about Buffalo but I knew what was on the other side.

"Hey Meg, have you ever seen Niagra Falls?"

She thought for a second and said "No, let's go there!"

I was once on a road trip with my dad to Toronto and he gave me the full tourist experience when he switched traffic lanes and said, "Look, there's Niagra falls!" But I thought it would be nice to see it closer than from the freeway.

We parked my car and started walking around. It really is a wonder to see the falls up close. We decided to take the tour so we got on "The Maid of the Mist". We donned our complimentary ponchos that were nothing more than plastic garbage bags with hoods on them. Megan and I laughed at everything on the tour. We were young, in love and 200 miles away from our neighbors. We had a blast!

Those ponchos don't really protect you from much and you'll be soaked wet as the boat takes you under and around one of the 7 wonders of the world. Take my advice and don't wear a white t-shirt and bra like

Megan did with her nipples exposed to 400 senior citizens on a tour ship around Buffalo! She was kind of embarrassed but she just rolled with it. In her defense, she was 21 years old and those boobs never looked better!

We checked into a hotel and put on some dry clothes. That night we went to the casino and had a nice dinner. It was one of the first times Megan and I had gone anywhere together and I remembered thinking I could spend the rest of my life with that woman. The next morning, I accidentally slammed the trunk of my car on her head as she was putting her bag in, but because I am so romantic I let her sleep off the concussion and I drove home.

Good Luck in Jail

I've worked from the time I was 13. I started at Dave's supermarkets and had a job all through high school. At the end of my senior year in 1994, I worked as a stock boy at the local K- Mart. It was an absolutely terrible job. I only took the job so I could steal cassette tapes from the electronics department but soon after I started, the switch to cds had taken over so they stopped bringing in any new tapes. My job was basically to wander the aisles and ask people if they needed help. I don't know how closely you have been following these stories but helping people is not exactly my bread and butter. I'm really more of a "Go fuck yourself" kind of guy.

There was a big K-mart company meeting before the Fourth of July where they notified all employees that they were closing the Collinwood location after Christmas of that year. They gave employees advanced warning so people could hurry up and use their vacation time before they transferred to another store. I didn't have a car or a license at the time so I was gonna be out of a job on Christmas. Part of me considered quitting right there at that meeting but seeing as how this was the third job I'd had in a year, I decided I'd stick it out and start looking for something better. That very same day, my manager told me I needed to work the upcoming Saturday even though I requested the day off weeks before. I was livid. The next day I was just going to tell my boss that I had plans I could not break and would indeed be taking Saturday off whether he liked it or not. As I walked up to work, I psyched myself up for the inevitable argument that would happen when I told my boss. I did some quick math in my head and realized if I had to, I would just quit. I had enough money in the bank to last me until I found a new job. If I was frugal, I figured I could go until after Christmas if I had to. I punched in and looked for my boss. I found out he had the day off and I was kind of disappointed. I thought about it all night and was ready to argue. I figured I could leave a note on his desk about it and argue tomorrow.

A nice older woman asked me to mix up some paint for her and I got to work. All the paint at K-mart was white, small doses of color had to be added to it to get whatever color you wanted. Then the can was put into this mechanical contraption that would shake the can vigorously for 2 full minutes. I put her first can in the mixer and we walked over to another aisle to find paint brushes she needed. When I heard the paint mixer stop, we walked back to switch out the cans. As we turned the corner I was shocked to see the most beautiful shade of light blue paint covering everything in sight. Looked like the calmest river of all time running directly through the hardware section. Someone who was still a novice at using the paint mixing machine had neglected to hammer the lid of the paint can back into place before putting it in the machine! I turned to the sweet old lady and said "Can you excuse me while I go find a manager?" I proceeded to the time clock, walked right past my manager, and punched the fuck out. Calmly, I walked out the back door of K-mart and never went back. For all I know, that lady is still waiting for me in aisle 17.

When Saturday rolled around I was ready to make the festival scene. WMMS the local radio station had switched over to an "alternative" format like a million other radio stations did in the wake of Nirvana and they had a big free all day concert at Nautica headlined by Green Day. I didn't care for most of the grunge wannabe bands on the bill but I did actually like Green Day. It was the summer of '94 and started to really blow up. They were already pretty popular and had a video getting heavy airplay on MTV. They were popular enough that you would tell people that you had seen them twice before anytime someone would mention them. Punk credibility was really important in the early 90's!

My friend Ed Boyle was the only one of us who had a car so Mike Diliberto, Chris Kulcsar, Joe Holzheimer and I piled into Ed's Charger and we rolled down to the Flats. We went pretty early because one of the first bands playing that day was a band we liked called Pansy Division. Pansy Division were an openly gay punk rock band who took special delight in getting knuckleheads and frat guys who were in the audience to start throwing things or become grossed out hearing songs about gay sex. (If you are in a large group of people and some Ohio State frat guy starts to be extra loud about how "disgusting" it is to see two men kiss, that guy is usually gay.) My friends and I had gathered near the stage and were being extra vocal in our support of the band. I liked the band already, but seeing squares flip them off made me want to cheer extra loud!

Someone in our group (probably Chris) had a permanent marker in their back pack and we started writing silly gay positive statements on ourselves, riot -grrl style. I wrote " QUEER-CORE 94" on my right forearm and Joe wrote "HOMO SEX AL" and drew a stick figure on my left shoulder when I had my sleeves pulled up. I wish I could remember what everyone else wrote on their arms because some of it was really funny. If you were actually gay and saw us you would probably think we were making fun of gay people but we genuinely meant it as a supportive gesture at the time. I'm sure we looked ridiculous no matter what our intent was. After Pansy Division's set ended Chris, Mike and Joe were gonna meet up with another group of our friends to skateboard around downtown. I wasn't a skateboarder at all, I learned the hard way that I just wasn't built for any kind of cube gleaming during a downhill disaster in my driveway a few summers prior to this. So Ed and I walked to the other side of the Flats where they had some kind of a rib burn-off to get some grub.

By the time the rest of the group had met up with us, the group had grown much larger. Rob Tepley, Grady Willrich, Matt Lanzeretta, Jim Kosem and others had come down for the free show. We had quite the crew gathered in the bleachers ignoring whatever band was playing. Rob's sister Laura Tepley and her friend Tia joined our group. I was in the middle of telling Grady some tale when Laura took off her t-shirt to reveal only a bikini top. Joe claims I stopped midsentence and my mouth just hung open staring at her. I don't remember all of that but I don't doubt it. Laura was always the hottest of any of our friends' siblings. (She had a crush on me since I was in seventh grade). The pavilion was extremely crowded by that point and most people had been out in the sun drinking overpriced beer since 2 in the afternoon. When the band Collective Soul started to play whatever you call their hideous music a change was noticeable throughout the crowd. What had been a pretty nice relaxed summer crowd started to become a surly, drunken sun-burned mass of human garbage as the sun went down.

Collective Soul finished boring people to death and played their one radio hit as a finale. We were relieved that they were done and the only band we came to see were on next.

There seemed to be a longer wait between bands than normal. After about 40 minutes, we started to hear people saying that Green Day cancelled and the show was over. The crowd chanted, "GREEN! DAY! GREEN! DAY! GREEN! DAY!" It's kind of a drag when a band you like starts getting popular and played on the radio but hearing thousands of sweaty meatheads chant their name was enough to make you hate them altogether. Through no fault of their own, I decided I no longer liked Green Day at that very instant. (Not true, but I stopped *admitting* that I still liked them for a few years.) Ed said we should probably get out of there as we started to notice a pretty thick police presence. Some radio station jerk-off came onstage flanked by two cops and announced, "Due to an over capacity venue the City of Cleveland and WMMS promotions have decided to end the show. We will re-schedule with the band to have them come back at a later date to play a larger venue. Please start to move in an orderly fashion to the exits at the back of the pavilion. We are sorry for any inconvenience this may have caused. Please keep your radio's locked to 100.7 WMMS the home of rock and roll in Cleveland!" Before he could finish saying the word Cleveland, he got hit square in the chest with a 9 dollar beer bottle.

A line of police in riot gear moved from the front of the stage, pushed the crowd back and more beer bottles, pop cans, Frisbees, and other assorted garbage started flying through the air toward Cleveland's finest. The police moved forward in a straight line almost like they had trained for this. Joe, Mike, Ed and I ran towards the exit, but it was like a herd of cattle trying to get through the two gates, I turned my head just in time to see my buddy Chris jump up and grab a light fixture with both hands and rip it off the wall. Chris was a pretty level headed guy so whatever that light fixture did to him you can be sure it deserved it. Before I could ask him what the hell he was doing two policeman grabbed Chris and put him in handcuffs. I ran back toward the cops and yelled, "He didn't do anything!" Then I was tackled from behind by Officer Roid-Rage who said, 'You want some too?" As several honorable officers of the law stood on my head and put my hands in cuffs I saw Chris Kulcsar perform 1 of the 3 greatest athletic feats I have ever witnessed. As soon as the two cops who were arresting him turned their attention to jumping on my back, Chris took off sprinting in the opposite direction with his hands in cuffs behind his back! One of the cops on top of me noticed and ran after Chris. He caught up to Chris and slammed him into a brick wall. Evidently, that tackle was caught by the Channel 19 Action News team and although I haven't seen the footage I was told that it was "gnarly".

Chris and I were led by cops to a paddy wagon and thrown inside where we were greeted by two other rioters. *One of whom would years later become the drummer in Chris and my band The Chargers! We didn't know Adam at the time but he assured us he was absolutely innocent.* It was my first time in a paddy wagon so I tried to throw off the intimidating silent vibe because I didn't know if I had to knife one of those guys yet. It was probably 11 o'clock on a hot July night and every 20 minutes or so the back door of the

meat wagon would swing open and two or three more
felons would be tossed in. It was sweltering inside
that windowless sweatbox and you could actually see
a small river of sweat draining down the aisle of the
truck. I was able to pull one of my wrists out of the
handcuffs because I was so sweaty, apparently I lost
weight! *And is there some cosmic rule that says when
your hands are placed in handcuffs you will have the
worst itch of all time somewhere on your body?* With
my free hand I was able to discreetly take care of said
itch on top of my head. I quickly put my hand behind
my back before anyone saw I was free and tried to
convince me to do something stupid like open the
door to the truck.

The back door swung open and they put two more
people in. There was no room on any of the benches so
they told the last two guys to sit on the floor in the
river of sweat for the ride to the station. Once the
paddy wagon started moving there was a small breeze
that came in from vents in the top of the truck. That
cool breeze lifted everyone's spirits and a few of us
started to make jokes about how silly it all was. By the
time we reached the police station I had convinced
myself we would all get tickets or something minor and
they would let us go. As usual, I was wrong. They led
us out of the truck and into a large holding cell where
one by one they questioned us. I was pulled out and I
sat at a desk with a cop and emptied my pockets. He
made a copy of my state ID and put all my belongings
into a plastic bag. The cop told me to take the laces out
of my shoes and put them in the bag.

"Why do you need my shoelaces?" I asked.

"So you don't hang yourself", the officer said without looking up from his paperwork.

Hang myself? All of a sudden it started to feel like I was actually in jail. Chris was still 17 so even though it was his fault that I was here, he was taken to a different room, shoelaces intact, where he was able to call his parents and have them come pick him up. I was taken to the drunk tank of the second district Cleveland Police station where I was told to sit tight and wait. The cell filled up with mostly the same guys in the paddy wagon with me. There were two older Puerto-rican dudes off in a corner sleeping it off and there was one large black man who kept making jokes about "ain't never seen this many white folks up in here!" This was very funny to him. The cell directly across from us was an all glass enclosure with a 40-ish near west side white guy who had a serious withdrawal situation. He laid on a blanket perfectly still then all of a sudden would let out a scream and his body would go into convulsions. I had never seen anything like this before. I was never going to be a drug user anyway but the image of that guy rolling around on the floor of a jail cell pops into my head whenever I hear the word *heroin*. My first trip to jail and I had been scared straight!

Who says there are no reform success stories?!

So other than not being dope sick in a solitary cell let's take stock of where I was. I was an 18 year old "adult" for a little more than two months and was already unemployed, broke, no girlfriend, no car, and lived at home with an alcoholic mother and boyfriend and now I was waiting for my one phone call in jail with the words "Queer-Core 94" written on my arm for everyone to see. You could say I had seen better days.... At least my good friend Homo-Sex Al was covered by my t-shirt, tight? It was important to stay positive during stressful times like those...

There are no clocks in a holding cell so I had no idea what time it was when they called my name to go talk to an officer. I was told that I was being charged with "disorderly conduct" and I had to appear in court on Monday morning. I was allowed one phone call to have someone come pick me up and since it was a misdemeanor there was no bail needed. I dialed my home phone number and said a silent prayer my sister Bel would pick up. She didn't. "Hello?' My mom mumbled after the 22nd ring.

"Mom, it's Lachlan. I got arrested and I need you to come pick me up at the second district on Lorain."

"DO YOU KNOW WHAT TIME IT IS?" I didn't, but she slurred her words a little, "What did you do?"

"I didn't really do anything, a bunch of people got arrested during a mini-riot at the Green Day show. It's all a big misunderstanding. You don't have to pay anything or bail me out. Can you just come and get me? I'll explain everything."

"They won't hold you forever." she said and hung up the phone.

I was shocked. I held the phone up to my ear until that loud busy tone started. I hung up the phone and told the officer my Mom said she wasn't coming to get me. The cop felt bad and asked if I wanted to call someone else but I couldn't think of anyone to call. The officer explained to me that I would have to go back and wait in the holding cell but they would release me at 7 am during the shift change. He let me use the bathroom and drink a glass of water before leading me back down to the cell. I sat on the bench in the holding cell as it emptied out one by one throughout the night. I don't know if I ever felt worse about myself in my entire life than I did that night. As I sat there staring off into space I made two very important promises to myself that I have been able to keep: I never asked my mother for a single thing after that day.

I promised to never go see Green Day in concert ever again, even if they were playing for free in my garage.

The policeman who felt bad for called my name just before 7 am and gave me a ride in his cruiser to Public Square. It was the nicest thing a policeman has ever done for me and I try to remember that when I am railing against cops. He said he had to go downtown for something and thought he would save me a trip because "the buses on Lorain are weird on weekends, you would have been waiting forever." I thanked him and walked toward the 39 bus stop so I could get home. Everyone was still sleeping when I walked in the door. I took the longest, hottest shower of my life to try to burn off the funk of sitting in jail all night in sweaty clothes. I scrubbed the marker off of my arms until my skin was raw. I just wanted to forget everything about the night before.

On Monday I went to the Justice Building bright and early. I saw a bunch of the same guys from Saturday night crowded around outside of the courtroom. I said, hi and one of the guys told me his lawyer agreed to defend all of us. I spoke to the lawyer and she explained we should plead not guilty to all charges and more than likely the city would just drop the charges to avoid going to a trial over misdemeanors. I asked her what it would cost me and she said since she was already there for her client she could bundle all of us into one fee and I would just pay my share of the fee. The more people we had on our side, the cheaper it would be for everyone. That sounded great but I didn't want to deal with a trial and have this thing linger over my head. As I considered her offer I walked around the corner to talk to a clerk and asked him how I go about speaking to a public defender. He told me public defenders will be assigned after we are arraigned. I wasn't sure what any of that meant. The clerk of courts gave me a handbook that explained how everything worked.

I sat in the courtroom listened to most of my jailhouse friends go up there and plead not guilty and then take a card from the lawyer lady on the way out the door. Something about the way she smiled when she handed out her business cards made me uneasy. Going to trial in hopes of getting charges dropped might work for these Chagrin kids and their parents lawyers friends but I didn' t have anyone on my side and I just wanted this whole thing behind me. When the judge called my name I plead, no contest. According to the handbook, I read that meant that I was admitting no guilt but that I would be willing to accept a punishment at the judge's discretion. The judge asked me if I was fully aware of what no contest meant for me.

"I believe I do." I said to him.

"Have you ever been arrested before Mr. MacKinnon? He asked. When I said no, he said, "Plea of No Contest accepted, 200 dollar fine and enrollment in the First Offense program recommended. Case dismissed." He slammed his gavel down.

I walked back to the clerk of courts with my paperwork and he explained I had 30 days to pay my 200 dollar fine plus 50 dollars in court costs and he gave me a different handbook outlining the First Offense program which basically meant that once I paid my fine I would be put on probation for one full year. As long as I was not arrested and I able to pass 12 monthly drug tests then my conviction would be expunged from my record. I figured a 250 dollar fine was not that big of a deal and if I tried really hard, I probably could stay out of jail for another year.

When I got home I took 250 dollars up to the store to get a money order so I could pay the fine that very day. I decided my plan of not working that summer had just been dealt a very serious setback so I started looking for a job a few days after. First I had to get a job, set up a bank account, get a license, buy a car, and move far, far away from Collinwood.

At least that was my plan.

The Worst Thing I Ever Did

I learned from a great Butthole Surfers record, it is always better to regret something you have done than something you haven't. That has always stuck with me and although I agree with that philosophy, the following story is one thing in my life that I wish I could take back. When I was about 11 years old I hadn't really noticed girls or become obsessed with rock and roll yet. I spent all of my time reading, watching, and learning about sports. I was the kid who could tell you Tony Gwynn's batting average in 1984 (.351) or how many sacks Lawrence Taylor had in 1986 (20.5). I read everything I could get my hands on about football, baseball or basketball and a lot of those stats just stuck in my head. I collected baseball and football cards obsessively. I am still upset my cousin Ian taped a Brian Sipe card to the spokes of his bike so it would sound like a motorcycle. We all did that but you weren't supposed to use football cards you were supposed to steal the aces out of a deck of playing cards or use the business card that lady from Child Protective Services gave you last summer! A pack of baseball cards cost 35 cents at the 7-11 by St. Jeromes so an enterprising young man like myself could usually come up with enough for a pack by looking under the couch cushions or under the floor mats of my mom's car.

Every now and then I could use my charm on my parents to weasel a couple of bucks out of them for doing some extra chores. I would take that two dollars and really treat myself at the baseball card shop in the neighborhood. Baseball Card Bonanza was a small storefront on the corner of Lucknow and E.152nd street. I loved that place, it was two blocks behind the school so sometimes after dismissal I walked over there to kill some time. I loved looking through the binders of old baseball cards in protective plastic sheets, it got to the point where I could tell each year by the style of the card at a quick glance. I would spend hours in there talking sports or immersing myself in issues of Sports Illustrated from the 70's. More important than all of that though it gave me a place to go after school that was all mine. There was zero chance of running into my sisters or anyone who knew my family in that shop.

After going in there a few times I struck up a friendship with the owner of the store Gil. Gil was a retired police officer in his mid to late 50's who was just as fanatical about sports as I was. He opened the store after doing 30 years on the police force more as an excuse to get out of the house than as a very profitable business. He made his real money at the track on Tuesdays and Sundays and for the record he always felt that Pete Rose got railroaded by the commissioner of baseball because as he would say, "Everybody bets on sports. That's big business!" Gil wanted to make sure that I was allowed to be hanging out in the shop all the time and he wouldn't believe me when I would tell him

that my mom didn't care as long as I was home before
the streetlights came on, so finally I told him to go
ahead and call my mom. I gave him my phone number
and he called her.

"Mrs..MacKinnon this is Gil from the Baseball Card
Bonanza on 152nd street. Lachlan has been
coming...No, no he isn't in trouble... No, nothing
like that, I just wanted to...oh ok, sure...I
understand...Sorry to bother you.." Gil hung up the
phone and looked me in the eyes and said "Lachlan,
You are welcome to hang out here for as long as you
like."

I laughed and said "told ya!" as I only imagined what
kind of nonsense he heard from my mother on the
other end of that phone call. I had told her where I
was going after school but she had my brother
Malcolm to worry about and as long as the police
weren't bringing me home she was fine with whatever
I was doing.

Since I was already hanging around the store so much
Gil decided to put me to work. He would buy entire
collections of cards from people pretty often and had
me do the tedious work of separating out these
collections. It was the kind of stuff that took a long
time and was boring for most people, but I absolutely
loved it. First I would separate all the baseball cards

from the football cards. Then I would take all the baseball cards and separate them by year putting each year's cards in order. Sometimes I had to go through an entire year's set and separate them all by team. Occasionally Gil would get a phone call from someone who was looking for all the Cleveland Indians players on 1963's Topps set and I would pull the 1963 box and I would get to work going through and pulling all the Indians out. At the end of the night before I left he would come up with a dollar amount that I had earned and he'd tell me, "Go ahead and grab 5 dollars' worth of cards" and I would very carefully start flipping through the binders. He had different binders separated by price, I usually stuck to the 25 cent binders but every now and then I would opt for quality over quantity. I picked an early Reggie Jackson card for a dollar. The most I ever spent was 7 dollars for Nolan Ryan's second year card.

After a couple of months, Gil realized I was really just avoiding going home and even though I was only 11. He could tell I was trustworthy enough to leave me in the store alone while he ran up to McDonald's to grab some lunch or run to the bank before they closed. It got to the point where he was comfortable enough to actually take an hour long lunch break on Saturdays while I covered the store. Gil didn't even have a cash register so he would leave me a five, four singles and four quarters to make change for anyone while he was gone. Anyone who needed more change than that would have to wait until Gil got back but I never ran into that. The store had a pretty small clientele and was mostly kids from the neighborhood spending less than 3 dollars at a time.

On Saturdays Gil would bring me back a cheeseburger and some fries from wherever he went and at the end of the night he started to give me a ride home to my house if it was close to getting dark. Once he let me come with him when he closed the store and drove to Mayfield to make an offer on someone's collection of football cards from the 70's. When we got to the guy's apartment he handed us 5 or six shoeboxes full of football cards and we started to look through them in his kitchen. Gil showed me how to go through them really fast and just pulled the superstars' cards. We looked for Mean Joe Green's, Roger Staubach's, Joe Namath's, and OJ Simpson's. All of the good to average players were considered junk. Gil explained every set only had 6 or 7 cards worth anything each year and even though he was going to make an offer on all of the cards, his offer was based on how many of those 6 or 7 we found. I felt like I had been given some kind of secret insider knowledge and it sometimes felt like we were partners. It was pretty cool, even though looking back on it now I did all of his grunt work and he would pay me in 5 dollars' worth of cards in exchange for 5 hours' worth of work......

My favorite thing to do when Gil left me alone in the shop was to open up the glass display case and look at some of the stuff in there up close. There was the high

dollar shit I could never afford. Where he kept the
Hank Aaron and Roberto Clemente rookie cards in
class holders. Where he had a football with all the
members of the 1964 NFL Champion Cleveland
Browns autographs on it (Fuckin Art Modell! signed
this ball directly under Jim Brown's
autograph....Jerk.). The coolest thing in the case was a
set of miniature baseball pennants with the numbers
of every player in the hall of fame from that team on
it. They were so cool. They were made in 1970 by the
RC Cola company as stadium giveaways so having
the complete set was probably next to impossible. He
was selling the set for 500 dollars but Gil told me that
really meant that he wanted to get 300 for it. I was
never a very big memorabilia guy but something
about these pennants were so cool to me. I'm not
proud of what I am going to tell you next but...

One day when Gil had to run to the bank I looked
through the pennants and I put the Yankees pennant
into my backpack and took it home. I thought about
this for many years, I still don't know what compelled
me to do it. One pennant out of the set was not going
to be worth anything but the whole set minus one
pennant was also not going to be worth anything. The
Yankees weren't even my favorite team (they were
second favorite to my hometown Indians, but the
Indians were always so terrible in the 80's that every
kid I knew had a back-up team to root for). I never
even hung the pennant up in my room because I was
sure my mom would take one look at it and know that
it was stolen!! I think when you grow up poor you

become a little more fixated on STUFF. All your clothes are hand-me-downs, all your toys are second-hand and had to be shared. The coolest thing about my baseball cards was no one in my family was even the least bit interested in them. They were just mine and I didn't have a whole lot of things that were just mine. Something about that pennant represented all the cool stuff in my life that I would never have. I don't know if I was thinking about that when I was 11 or if I am just trying to justify it to myself 30 years later, but stealing that pennant still bothers me.

About a year after my heist I walked into the shop after school just like I had been doing and I noticed Gil in a bad mood. Gil was never in a bad mood. I figured he had a bad day at the track or something so I just tried to stay out of his way. He moved a bunch of stuff around in the display case and I started to get worried. It had been so long ago I forgot about stealing that Yankees pennant. Gil knew that I loved that set of pennants and he asked, "Did you ever look through these pennants and maybe take them out of order? I had a guy looking at them today, but I am missing the Yankee pennant?"

"No, I never took them out of order. I looked through them before and the Yankees pennant was in there." I said.

"Well, it's not here now!" He said angrily. Gil turned to face me, "I have been thinking, I really can't have you hanging around the shop anymore. You are the only other person who could have gone into this case and that missing pennant just cost me 500 dollars! We don't make a ton of money here. You can't do this to me!"

I was caught. He knew it by the look on my face. I just said "I'm sorry" and ran out of the store. I cried the entire walk home. I did something so stupid. The only thing Gil had ever been for me was a good friend and I repaid him by stealing from him. My heart sank because there was no way I could ever make it up to him, he was never going to trust me to watch the store for him again. I waited until after I knew that the store was closed for the night and I took that stupid pennant, put it in a big manila envelope with a note that said "I'm really sorry" in it and I put it through the mail chute in the front door.

A few weeks later I got a job as a paperboy for the Euclid Sun Scoop. The scoop was a neighborhood paper that came out once a week and my route just happened to include Lucknow. Every Thursday after school I would deliver the paper to the 4 blocks on my route and every week I would slide a paper through Gil's door even though he had no subscription. Gil would sometimes see me and nod from behind the counter but I never got the courage to go back in the store and talk to him. As the neighborhood changed, he eventually closed down the shop as less and less kids were interested in collecting little cardboard pictures of Jose Canseco. He was gone before I quit that stupid paper route the next summer and I never spoke to him again. I still have my baseball card collection in a box in my attic but every time I think that I should go through them to try to sell some I think of that look on Gil's face the last time I was in his store and I decide not to bother.

I'm really sorry, Gil.

Big Brother Blues

In all fairness I would have to admit that I was a pretty terrible older brother to my sister Morrighan. She is my Irish twin, born just 15 months after I was and I guess I was pissed that I never got a whole lot of time to enjoy being the bab y. In large families there is always weird issues revolving around where you fit in among your siblings, There was also the fact that I had an older brother that was always messing with me and beating me up and when Morrighan came along I got to take all the frustrations I had with Warburton out on her. It's not cool and I'm sorry but this is what happens with feral children, Didn't you ever read Lord of the Flies?? Anyway I didn't act alone, my sister Belphoebe was usually right by my side as we tortured our poor, helpless middle sister. Since Bel was 2 years older, she should have stopped me but she didn't. It's really HER fault!

Every time a new sibling was born in my family while I was growing up there would be a weird adjustment period where everyone's bedrooms switched around to make room for the new tenant. My sister Feowyn was born on Christmas in 1982, so for a year or two I shared a bedroom with both Bel and Morrighan. Warburton moved up to the attic. My parents had a room and the baby had a room. Although the house was pretty big, our room was incredibly crowded once three beds was in it. Our house had those old fashioned radiators in it and the radiator in our room had a little cup sort of attached to the top of it, You could put a little water in it during the winter and the radiator would add moisture to the air, I am guessing they did this to combat the dreaded winter itch but I am not a mechanic so what the hell do I know about radiators? What I do know is that one night my Mom put some water in that cup and a few hours later it started making a little hissing noise. Morrighan woke up in the middle of the night and got freaked out by the noise so she got up and went to sleep with my mom.

The next morning at breakfast she was still scared about the noise that Bel and I slept right through, we both assured her that she was crazy and went off to school not thinking about it. That night as we were getting ready for bed, My mom put water in the radiator cup (by the way, I'm sure that radiator cup IS the technical term for this part, so get off my back Home Depot) and we went to sleep. A few hours later Morrighan woke us up again, "Guys, do you hear that? It's like a whistle or something...what is it?"

Being the shitty brother that I am I said 'Go back to sleep!" but Bel was far more evil and she said, "I hear it too .... It' s like a hiss.... Like a ghost or something" And then she turned on the juice" This noise is really FREAKING ME OUT!!!"

Morrighan got up immediately and ran to Mom's room, I wasn't positive, but there was a good chance that she was crying. Bel rolled over and called to me ,'That noise is just the radiator right?"

"Yeah, I think it's just steam from that cup."

After school the next day, Bel told me Morrighan liked sleeping in Mom's room and we both laughed. Morrighan was not having a good week. After dinner, we noticed she had the worst case of blood shot eyes I'd ever seen. She nursed her milk pretty hard and she was already worried about not getting any sleep for the third night in a row. Since I am such a swell guy I said to her, "Hey Mo, that hissing in our room? It's just steam coming out of the radiator. I will tell mom not to fill up that cup tonight and I bet there won't be any noise at all."

Bel was livid! She was shooting me an evil look but I had a plan. I waved Bel's dirty look off and I reassured Morrighan that everything would be ok.

Before we went to bed that night I peeled the paper off of a red crayon and broke it into tiny pieces. I put the crayon in the radiator cup with a tiny bit of water but I made sure not to tell my sisters. Morrighan made Mom promise that she would not put any water in the radiator when we went to sleep that night. Morrighan narc' d out as soon as her head hit the pillow but sure as shit she woke up a few hours later in a panic, "There' s that noise again! Bel, wake up do you hear it?"

"Yeah, I hear it too . It's worse than before though.....Lachlan, is that coming from the radiator?" she asked.

I rolled over and said, "Mom promised she didn't put water in it tonight.....what is that noise? Sounds like it's bubbling almost......"

'Oh my God, I'm getting Mom. I think we have a ghost!!" Morrighan yelled.

"WAIT! Mom is getting pissed about this." Bel pointed out to us, "Lachlan, turn on the light."

I got out of bed and walked over to the light switch, as soon as I flipped the lights on all of our eyes fixed on the radiator where the red crayons had now melted and run down the radiator.

"THE RADIATOR IS BLEEDING!!!!" I yelled.

Morrighan let out a scream that could be heard on Lake Shore Boulevard and ran as fast as she could out of the room crying! My mom ran into our room took one look at the radiator and said "This shit is not funny! And you better clean that up!

For future reference, it's really hard to scrape off dried red wax from a steel radiator and even more impossible to get it off of blue carpet .

To this day I don't know if Morrighan has forgiven us, but I feel like I did her a big favor because the wax from the crayon totally broke that radiator cup so although we all were victims of severe winter itch we never had to listen to Morrighan cry about the whistling noise in the middle of the night again. My parents made me move up to the attic to share a room with my brother soon after this, and if you thought a whistling radiator was bad, try going to sleep while your older brother tells you that he is going to murder you and then puts on Echoes by Pink Floyd every night for a year.

Cleveland Public Power

Megan and I have a re-occurring discussion about our 10 year old son Declan and whether or not he is old enough to stay home alone sometimes. I try really hard not to compare his childhood to mine. Obviously, I had to deal with things that he will never even have to think about, and that's a good thing . I know that times have changed but both Megan and I grew up in the eighties. We were part of the latch key kid generation, Well she was, I never had a key to my house because the door was never locked.

I remember one Friday during the summer of 1986. I was ten years old, The same age as my son is now. My Mother left the house with Morrighan to go up to the Salvation Army to watch my other sister Bel's softball game. I was gonna stay home and watch my brother Malcolm who was still a baby because he was napping and my mom didn't want to wake him up to take him to the game. Mom told me that he would probably sleep until she got home so really, all I had to do was hang out with my four year old sister Feowyn MacKinnon while she watched a movie.

This kind of thing happened all the time and it wasn't until I was older that I found out that not everyone grew up changing their younger siblings diapers. The point is, it was normal to us.

Most of the time, my older sister was home, and she was 12 so she knew what she was doing. On this particular Friday evening my brother woke up not ten minutes after my mom left and he was pissed! He was probably teething or something because I remember that none of my normal 10yr old Dad tricks were working to calm him down.

As I was about to get him a bottle there was a loud knock on our front door. Feowyn was absolutely no help because she was sitting in front of the TV with a big ass bowl of Golden Grahams and she did not move. I ran over to answer the door to find a guy from Cleveland Public Power holding a clipboard on the porch.

Poor Kid Pro Tip: Clipboards = Trouble. The service guy asked me if my parents were home and I guess the 10 year old holding a screaming baby wasn't a big eno ugh clue that NO. Clearly my parents were not home.

"Do you have anyone you can call? I have a shut off notice for your electricity and I have to cut your service unless you can pay the bill right now" he explained.

"Well, how much is it?" I asked, knowing that the eleven dollars I had hidden under my Sports Illustrateds probably would not cover it.

"It looks to be about 140 dollars, but I can keep it on if you pay 80 right now."

I don't have that kind of cash here. Are you sure you can't come back later, when my Mom is home?"

"Listen, Kid I am gonna have to turn it off but tell your Mom to call this number as soon as she gets home and I can swing by and turn you back on...."

As he walked back to his truck, I followed him, barefoot, still holding a crying infant and I turned on the juice.

"Hey Mister- My Mom will pay this as soon as she gets home, I promise! But you can't turn off the electricity on a kid! It's Friday and if you turn it off now we are gonna be without power all weekend (true) and if we have no power my little brother's monitor won't work (false, he didn't have monitor). C'mon, Mister have a heart!" and I gave him dome puppy dog eyes...

At just the right moment Feowyn yelled for me because she spilled her cereal on the carpet in the living room...

The service guy got back in his truck with his clipboard, handed me a copy of the shut off notice and said "I have to come back on Monday...Tell your Mom!" and he drove away.

Malcolm stopped crying as soon as we went back inside. Fe just put a dishtowel down on the carpet over her spill and we went back to watching whatever we were into that night.

Mom brought home some pizza a few hours later. Nice little weekend we had...

The St. Valentine's Day Massacre of 1993

The St. Valentines Day Massacre of 1993 started out innocently enough. It was a Sunday morning at my first job. I was a bag boy at Dave's super markets. Working at Dave's was like a rite of passage for kids who grew up in Collinwood. I got hired there my freshman year of high school by forging my mothers name on a work permit that said I was allowed to work as many hours as possible. I needed the cash and my mom certainly would not mind me being out of the house most of the time. It was actually a pretty decent job too, I was in the union pulling down a respectable 3.85 an hour! Plus, most of my friends worked there and the schedule was flexible enough for anyone . In hindsight, working until 10pm on school nights probably wasn't good for my GPA like my daily naps during Algebra.

After being there for a few years and showing them how reliable I was, I was put on the Sunday Morning opening crew that meant I had to open the store at 7 am. So I had to wake up by at least 640 so I could throw on a tie and run the 5 blocks to the store. It made Saturday nights a drag sometimes but I honestly didn't mind.

On Valentine's day, I woke up to a serious blizzard, the kind where snow us measured in feet not inches. When we got the store opened we realized that we were gonna be twidling our thumbs until we could go home at 1pm because the store was DEAD. No one was going to leave their house to go grocery shopping in this mess unless it was absolutely necessary.

The bakery at our store always made 3 times as many donuts on Sundays than they did during the week. At about 10 am the head baker Ralph came and told us bag boy s that they had a ton of special cherry glazed Valentine's Donuts that obviously were not gonna sell so he said "You guys go eat a few if you want."

I think by now you all know my position on free donuts! So we ran into the back of the bakery to see what we had to work with. Ralph showed us an entire bakery rack filled with fresh, free, delicious donuts. I can still taste them...

My friend and fellow bored bag boy Mike Partlow asked, "How many of these do you think you could eat before 1pm?"

"All of them!" I said.

BULL. SHIT. I got ten dollars here that says you can't eat more than I can."

"CHALLENGE ACCEPTED!"

We laid down some rules and got another bag boy named Ray to be our official scorekeeper. You had to eat and swallow the donut in front of Ray and if you puked you were out. These donuts were smaller than normal so we both ate 6 real quick and then got back upfront by the registers. Even though the store was dead, there was still some work to do, so we would keep making trips back to the bakery to eat a few then you would have to walk back upfront to work.

This went on for a few hours. I'd eat 6, he'd eat 6, I'd eat 4, he'd eat 4. By noon I ate 22 donuts and Mike was at 19 but he kept talking shit to me about how he "was just getting warmed up" and I got a little worried because as I was eating my 24th donut I kind of felt like I was gonna throw up and I didn't have 10 bucks to give him. At 12:30 Ray told me Mike just tied it up at 24 a piece.

I was pissed and I was sick of these fucking donuts! I summoned all the intestinal fortitude I could find and I choked down 3 more donuts before I waved the white flag. Mike came back there and as he was eating his 25th donut he gave up and handed me a ten dollar bill. I was the champion at last!!

 As I walked home from work I hurled 27 donuts worth of pink cherry flavored vomit up in the alley by East. 156th street. I went home feeling much better and immediately took a serious nap.

I have never been able to find these donuts again. They were so delicious!

It was worth it.

THE GREAT DEPRESSION

B eing funny is a defense mechanism. It is much easier to make a joke and change the subject than it is to tell people how you are really feeling about something. Behind every great comedian is usually massive amounts of pain and insecurity. It is the same feeling that leads all those great comedians to lifelong struggles with drugs or alcohol when they get off stage. I am no great comedian but I have been told that I am a funny guy. I hope you laughed a few times while reading this book because there are no laughs in this story. Just like great comedians, behind every legendary forklift operator, there is a story of pain, insecurity, and depression. This is my story.

In 2005, I was hired on at The Sanson Company, a produce wholesaler in Cleveland. It was a good, solid union job with good benefits and great Christmas bonuses. For an unskilled guy like myself, it was probably as good as it was going to get. The only drawback to the job was the hours were terrible. It was in the middle of the night, six days a week. On the one hand, it meant never seeing my wife or friends but on the other hand, all that overtime meant I no longer had to drive a cab on weekends. You take the good with the bad.

When my son Declan was born in September of 2006, I switched my schedule from starting at 3 am to 11 at night so that I could get home by 8 or 9 in the morning and spend all day with him while Megan went to work. I knew it would be hard on me physically but it was a small price to pay to spend that much quality time with him as a baby. My biggest fear about having kids was that I would miss out on watching him grow up because I had to work. Like, I would come home from work one day and he'd be in high school. At the time, the schedule and job seemed like a godsend. I don't know when the last time you went and priced out day care was but it is crazy expensive! Who wants to work all those hours just to be able to afford to pay someone else to raise your kids? I hated everything about the thought of daycare even more than the thought of diapers and I find diapers to be absolutely ridiculous! Diapers are so expensive and when you realize that you are spending that amount of money on shit, it is enough to make you go insane! You are literally flushing money down the toilet. We had our dog Ramona for about 5 years when Declan was born and she only ever had two accidents in the house? I was gonna let the dog potty-train Declan but my wife informed me that letting a toddler scratch at the side door and poop in the backyard is frowned upon.

I never could get used to working nights and sleeping during the day. I have always had trouble sleeping. Trying to do it when really exhausted and the sun is shining, people are mowing lawns, and kids are playing is next to impossible. I usually got a solid 3 maybe 4 hours of sleep at night. I could count on Declan napping with me for an hour or two in the afternoon but that was it. This went on for years.

I would ask around at work to see what they did and everyone had little tricks they would do to try to get some sleep, The thing that seemed to work best for longtime Sanson employees was to start drinking heavily as soon as one got off work in the morning. Hopefully one would pass out by 2 in the afternoon and you could get 10 solid hours of rest before the shift started at midnight. If one did a line of cocaine in one's car before one punched in, one would be wide awake and ready to face another night. There was an employee who got both of his kids prescriptions for Adderall and one could buy that for 2 dollars a pill if one were dragging. I could not handle any kind of uppers. I took an Adderall with a Coca-Cola during my 2 am lunch break one night when I was hurting and I didn't sleep a wink for 3 days! That shit was not for me. And since I don't drink I had to just try to rely on my own tricks. I cut out all caffeine, would never eat anything in the afternoon and try to black out all of my windows as best I could. If things got real bad, I would take a sleeping pill but I hated to do that because it was hard for me to wake up afterward.

Another big drawback to a job like that is no one is really getting enough sleep, so EVERYONE is in a shitty irritable mood all the time. I didn't really realize how bad it was until I didn't work there anymore. In the thick of it, I took for granted everyone called everyone else asshole or cocksucker or shit for brains. It had a real negative effect on the whole crew but seemed normal at the time. Everyone in the whole industry was wound too tight and burned out. People at Sanson had heart attacks in their early forties, it always felt like someone was putting a lot of pressure on you to get things done. No matter how much you did, there was always more to be done. People worked a ton of overtime to try to keep up, coming in on your one day off a week was pretty common. It felt like weird, macho bullshit to me. Guys bragged about working 70 hours a week or 22 days straight, like there was some kind prize to be had. I tried to avoid killing myself. It was nice knowing that I had to leave at 8 am so I could hang out with my buddy and watch Sesame Street.

Things got a little easier to deal with once Declan started school. I got home in the morning just in time to get him some breakfast and off to school on time. Once I dropped him off I would go home, make myself something to eat, clean up around the house and go to bed. But the sleep would not come. I found myself just lying in bed for hours getting frustrated and not sleeping. Nothing seemed to work and I was spending more time than ever in bed TRYING to sleep. I would block out 12 hours and only be able to sleep for 3. Some nights I would just get up and go hang out with Megan or let her get some sleep. We were on such opposite schedules that it was like we were both single parents. I took Declan to swimming

lessons during the day and Megan took him to karate
at night. When Sundays rolled around we tried to
have family time but I fell asleep at 3 in the afternoon.
I felt guilty when I was with them because I was so
out of it and I felt guilty when I was at home trying to
sleep because I was missing out on things. I just
couldn't win.

When I was growing up no one in my family went to
therapy or saw a professional to talk about things. Therapy
wasn't even mentioned as a possibility. We just weren't that
kind of family. My mom drank to cover up whatever she
was dealing with. My dad worked all the time. No one ever
talked to us kids about what was going on, so if any of us ever
had issues we dealt with them in whatever ways we could.
My older brother drank pretty heavy when he got out of the
Marines. Both Bel and Morrighan drank through high school,
not in a way that led to them having a problem but enough
to notice. I noticed when I got really stressed out I ate
impressive/disgusting amounts of fast food. I would swallow
my emotions like a good Irish Catholic and I would get on
with my day. I always felt since I didn't drink or do drugs
than I must have had a pretty good handle on things. I was
aware of being "bummed out" but I never missed work or
drank so it couldn't have been that bad, right?

Around 2012, Megan started to notice a significant change in
my mood and convinced me that maybe I should go talk to
someone and see if it would help? Because she was so
concerned I figured that I would go see someone, more to

please Megan than for myself. After talking to a psychologist, we figured I was probably suffering from depression and I probably suffered from it all my life. My Mom probably had it along with other members of my family but we just didn't recognize it. I guess it was hard to notice the symptoms if one was drunk every day. I was put on a low dose of an anti-depressant and there was a giant change almost immediately. I couldn't believe the difference and I thanked Megan for making me go. All of a sudden I was sleeping a little bit better, Still not as well as I'd like but better. I didn't feel like I should spend 23 dollars at Taco Bell for lunch and I dealt with the assholes at my job a little easier.

Sanson hired more people and we had a pretty reliable crew. I started taking a day off of work during the week along with Sundays. There was usually nothing fun to do on a Tuesday night so I got to have a nice dinner and spend a little time with my family. When they went to sleep I watched a movie or listened to records for a few hours. I found out that if I took 2 or 3 Vicodins I would get a really great night of sleep and I wouldn't be tired at all when I woke up. Because they were relatively easy to come by at work and not too expensive, I developed a little Tuesday night habit of putting on a Neil Young record on my headphones, popping a couple of Vics and drifted away into dreamland. I didn't even consider it as getting high. I just knew my favorite CDs sounded better and I was able to sleep for a solid 10 hours on my night off. As far as drug use went, it was pretty low-key. I never really told anyone and never did it anywhere but in my bedroom. I occasionally woke up on Wednesday and looked at my phone to see 37 texts I didn't remember sending but that was the extent of it.

In the summer of 2013, the owner and CEO had a bunch of meetings and shuffled people around. They made me the manager of the receiving department and gave me a raise. Things were looking good.

Being the manager of the department I already worked in didn't really change a whole lot for me. I was responsible for making the schedule and covering shifts if people called sick but that was all stuff that I already had a small hand in anyway. The only real change was I had to deal with the supervisors of different departments more often and that sucked. Each one of those department heads were usually more miserable than the next. On a company our size shit rolled downhill and receiving was at the bottom of the hill. If the shipping departments trucks didn't get out on time they would blame it on receiving. If a customer was there to buy something that a department head already sold, They would blame it on receiving. All the guys who were managers before me warned me about it but there wasn't a whole lot I could do about it, sometimes you just had to eat shit and smile.

I still took the anti-depressants but noticed myself slipping back into old habits. I couldn't sleep again. I ordered more fast food and Tuesday night Vicodin parties became Saturday night parties as well. I justified it by telling myself I needed the sleep. I saw friends less and less. I stopped playing guitar. All the time I spent with my family didn't make me feel any better. Megan mentioned it to me but I just thought that I was letting my frustrations at work get the best of me. I learned since that kids who grow up in alcoholic homes often have a hard time taking stock of how they are doing. They are so focused on other things around them they learn to put their own feelings off to the side. I think that's what I was doing around this time. I just kept telling myself as long as I wasn't drinking and I was still going to work, things would work themselves out.

My mood didn't improve over the winter and early into 2014, I was short with the guys on my crew if I spoke to them at all. I looked forward to my nights off so I could take my "medicine" and get some sleep. I never spent any time with Megan and if I did, we seemed to get on each others nerves. Declan was in school all day and a lot of times it felt like I was a third wheel when I was around. He and I didn't have our naptimes or our daily routine anymore. I didn't realize it at the time but I just missed them both so much and I didn't see any way to get to see them more often. When I would get a chance to stop and think about it, it bummed me out even more. Megan woke me up one night for work and asked me if I showered that day. I couldn't remember.

I felt like I had been lied to about how being an adult was going to work. I knew when I spent my 20s touring in a rock and roll band instead of going to college it would mean I would have to work harder for less. I understood that I was making that choice when the band broke up and my band mates went back to school. There was nothing I wanted to study. I had no passion for schooling and to me it seemed like it would be a colossal waste of time and money. Long ago, I made peace with that fact. But there should still be a place for the rest of us uneducated rubes to make a living. I got married before we had kids, bought a house had a decent job and a little money in the bank before we had kids. I was led to believe that this is how it should be done. But I was stuck in a job that was slowly killing me. They voted out our union, the neighborhood where I bought my house started to go to shit. I paid the mortgage late that year after Christmas so I was a month behind with new fees and penalties every week. On top of it all, my anti-depressants didn't seem to work anymore and I never got to see the two people in the world I most wanted too.

When they say depression is a mental illness they are not lying. From the time I was 19 years old whenever I was too angry or stressed out about something I could always count on Megan to put her arms around me and tell me things would be ok. I would feel better, even when I didn't really believe her. Something about her telling me things would be ok reassured enough for me. But when I was stuck in this depression I thought maybe SHE was the cause of it. The brain starts to play tricks on you and when the things that used to cheer you up no longer do, you start to take it out on those closest to you.

I got upset at some little thing like her not rinsing out a pan from dinner the night before and as I stood at the sink doing the dishes my head told me maybe if she just rinsed out this pan then I wouldn't be so angry right now! Everything started to become a trigger everything made me mad. The things that used to comfort or relax me now just made me irritable or upset. It's a scary thing when you can't trust your brain. Nothing made sense anymore and there was a small part of me that I knew I was acting and thinking irrationally but I couldn't stop it. That's the hardest part of my depression to explain to other people is the feeling of being out of control in your head. I would lie in bed unable to summon enough energy to take a shower but my head threw a thousand different thoughts a minute. I questioned everything. Heads became tails, true became false, and love started to feel like hate.

At the end of a shift one night, I sat in the shipping office with a couple of guys and the shipping manager Dan. Some of the issues I had in receiving were usually the result of Dan telling supervisors different stories. It was all too easy for him to cover for one of his trucks being late by saying they were waiting to get items off of new trucks in receiving. I thought Dan was kind of smarmy. The kind of guy who would think nothing about throwing someone else under the bus to make him look better. Other than that, he was a good guy, and we generally got along. He spoke to a newer driver in the office and the driver said something like "Well, it's just a bunch of niggers over there" and the guys in the office laughed. I waited until the drivers left and I said to Dan, "You can't let these guys talk like that and laugh about it."

"He was just joking, he didn't mean anything by it." Dan said.

"I don't care if he is joking or not. It's 2014 you can't drop N-bombs in front of your boss and get away with it!"

Dan got kind of pissed that I told him how to handle his crew. It probably wasn't my place but that kind of talk used to drive me insane. We were at East 37th and Woodland and only had employed about 6 black guys.

Out of 100 employees in the heart of the ghetto there were 6 black guys and none of them were managers. I heard the way people talked around work and it bothered me. I don't know what compelled me to say something to Dan about it but I felt better after I did. I figured it would be just like every other thing I ever said him and it would go in one ear and out the other. I didn't think anything of it until the next night when a couple of the black guys cornered me and asked me about what happened. So obviously there was gossip about it. I specifically didn't say anything to Dan until the other drivers were out of the office in hopes of avoiding just this type of high school bullshit. That night Dan avoided eye contact with me and at 6 am I was told to go meet with the CEO Sam at 730 am. I didn't think I was in trouble for anything.

When I walked into Sam's office he asked me if I thought the company was racist. I told him that that wasn't the issue. I told him I thought the company probably was racist and maybe that is why all but one department heads were Italian and only had a handful of black people working there. I also told him even if a company is racist you shouldn't be allowed to use the N word in front of your boss!

"So what would you like me to do?" Sam said.

"I don't know if you have to do anything other than tell Dan if his drivers are using racial slurs around him, maybe just don't laugh." I honestly couldn't believe we had that conversation. Sam went on to tell me that using the N word does not make people racist and that "every rap song has 40 N words in it." I tried in vain to explain to him it was a matter of respect we were talking about. It was just good manners to try not to throw out racial slurs at work! But he didn't see my point at all. He started to tell me all about my attitude problems and how no one likes me. All things that were absolutely true but still had no bearing on what we were talking about. He said "We just don't know if you are Sanson material, Lachlan. We are gonna let you go."

I didn't understand what he was saying. "What do you mean let me go?" I asked. "You're letting me go???!!!" I was stunned.

"We think you are a great worker but you are not a team player, maybe you'd be happier somewhere else." Sam offered.

"NOW!! Now I'm not a team player? You just promoted me and gave me a raise?? But now I'm not a team player???" I was in shock. "I have been here for 9 years! Almost 10! But all of a sudden NOW I'm not a team player........?????"

Sam spoke to me about a new opportunity and how they would be happy to write a recommendation. He couldn't have someone down on the floor stirring up trouble and calling the company racist. I told him that firing someone for asking a manager to stop using the N word is a real funny way of proving that your company was NOT racist! I'm not sure Sam heard anything that I said. A decision had been made and no amount of perfectly logical or salient points were gonna change his mind. Sanson's bottom line was more important than mine. Sam reached out to shake my hand, I said "Fuck you" and walked out the door. I was perfectly calm but I felt like I wanted to cry.

I walked out to my car in stunned silence. I knew exactly what I was going to do. I went home and picked up Declan. I gave him an extra big hug when I dropped him off at school, then I calmly drove to CVS and bought the two biggest bottles of sleeping pills they sold. I went home, took a shower and ate 200 sleeping pills along with the rest of the bottle of anti-depressants I had. I put on my headphones and I went to sleep.

It's hard to explain what I was thinking that morning and have it make sense because it doesn't make any sense at all. I have never been suicidal. No matter how bad things have ever been for me I never thought that it would be better if I were dead. I had been fired from jobs before but I always expected it or at least deserved it. This hit me out of the blue and at some point on my drive home from work it just made sense in my head. I knew it would be tough on my family but I figured in the long run both Megan and Declan would be better off. I had life insurance and I figured this would look like an accident. I felt bad about leaving Declan to grow up without a father but I worried that growing up around a depressed loser like me wasn't doing him any good either. When one gets a flat tire, one puts on the spare and keeps driving. I honestly felt like that was all I was doing that morning, fixing a problem. I know how crazy that sounds, I spent a lot of time thinking about the morning of March 6th, 2014.

I sat on my bed swallowing handfuls of pills perfectly calm. It didn't feel like a rash, emotional decision to me. It felt like a reasonable, logical solution to all of my problems and when I think back to that morning that is what scares me the most. It would be so much easier to justify it by saying "I was out of my mind" or "I was losing it" but my nervous breakdown didn't play out like I had seen them play out in movies. It was a strange morning, I don't know if I'll ever make sense of it.

I woke up in a hospital bed six days later. I don't remember anything about those six days at all and I am glad for that. I can tell you I did not see any bright white light. I did not have any grand visions or moments of clarity.

When I woke up I immediately remembered what put me in the hospital and my heart sank. However low you are feeling the day you decide to kill yourself I can promise that you will feel even worse the day you realize you were unsuccessful. Megan was by my side for all three days and when I woke up she explained that she heard me thrashing around up in my bedroom that night so she went upstairs and she could tell something was wrong. She called 911 and they rushed me to the hospital where they put me into a coma. Apparently if you take 200 sleeping pills the effect it has on you is very similar to a PCP overdose, so I was treated for a drug overdose instead of a suicide attempt. When I was awake and cognizant of what I had done, we asked to speak to a psychiatrist at the hospital but they never came.

Megan told me everything was going to be alright, We were gonna move-in with her mother and I would find a new job. That night I convinced her to go home and get some sleep. I sat in a hospital room and I stared at the ceiling for hours. I re-played what had brought me to that point and the truth is that nothing changed. If anything it was worse because I had yet another failure hanging over my head. As I sat in that hospital bed I started to see clear and relatively easy solutions for each one of our problems. I wasn't feeling better but I wasn't quite so hopeless either. I wish I could tell you that I had some epiphany in that hospital bed but I'm not sure that ever happens. What I did decide was to give things another shot. If not for me, then at least for Megan's sake.

The next morning they let me go home. I walked out of the hospital into a blizzard. I have often made jokes in the past about how I would love to go into a coma for a few days, but I have to tell you that when you wake up from a coma, you are not refreshed at all. You're just tired. Step one for me was to talk to a doctor about my depression. We went and saw my psychologist and I convinced her that I desperately did not want to go back on medication. I told her that I had used the anti-depressants as a quick fix and I wanted to try to figure things out on my own before deciding to go back on them. She disagreed but said as long as I would go to therapy then she would trust me. I tried therapy in the past and I didn't get much out of it. I never felt better after talking about my past, I usually felt worse. But I gave it another chance. The woman I went to see helped me to see things a little differently and I found for the first time talking helped my mood.

Step two was to find a job. My friend Pam and her dad had a landscaping business and she agreed to pay me under the table for the summer until I found something better. That gave me about 4 or 5 weeks until the season started. I really appreciated not being forced to go to job interviews right out of the gate. It would give me a little time to figure other things out. Step three was to get caught up on bills. I was going to take some money out of my 401k account and I sold my record collection. It was painful but I figured that I got us into this mess so I had to get us out of it. I called my friend Charles and without even looking he gave me 3 grand. It meant we could keep our house. It felt like it was the least I could do for Megan. I ended up selling the records for about a dollar a piece and I'm sure Charles made a small killing on some stuff. I could have made much more if I sold the records online but it was an emergency and I needed it done fast before I changed my mind. That Mudhoney record wasn't gonna sound so great if I was homeless, so I told myself that CDs sound just as good and moved on. If you bought any of my amazing used records at My Mind's Eye in the spring of 2014, you can be sure your money went to a good cause. My friend Jacob helped me get some much needed breathing room when he sold my Ozzie Newsome jersey online a couple weeks later.

Slowly, but surely I was able to get things in order. I had to stop going to therapy when our insurance ran out. The day after I went in to the hospital Megan called a co-worker of mine and she started to piece together what happened. In yet another example of how great she is, she called Sam and told him that I tried to kill myself because he fired me unjustly and he better keep me on the payroll until I at least get out of the hospital! I was in a coma at the time, so I don't know if she threatened to burn his house down or not but whatever she said worked because we never got a bill for my stay at the hospital AND I got paychecks for the 4 weeks of vacation time I was owed. People often talk about rehab or recovery like it's this thing that everybody gets but the truth is, most people can't afford to get help.

If heroin is easier to get than insurance then there isn't much of a choice at all.

I can never thank Megan enough for sticking by me through the whole thing. It certainly was enough to kill even the most solid of relationships. Her brother was getting married the weekend after I fucked everything up and she was supposed to be in Hawaii with my mother-in-law at the wedding. Probably the thing I feel the worst about is that she missed that trip to stay in a hospital room to watch me sleep. I always feel guilty about it when I am around my brother-in-law Patrick (good thing he lives in Hawaii...) One small bright spot is that my mother-in-law Barbara took Declan in Meg's place so while Megan and I dealt with the worst week of our entire lives, my son got to be the best man at his Uncle Pat's wedding! Not many 7 year old kids get to go on vacation to Hawaii and I feel a tiny bit less horrible about the whole episode when he tells me about how much fun he had. We tried to hide what I was going through the best we could but kids pick up on things. Most of the stories in this book involve things my parents were trying to hide from me! We told him I had a bad reaction to some new medicine I was taking and that it was an accident but he was at home when paramedics carried me out of the house. How can you make up for something like that?

In August of 2014, I got hired at Amresco in Solon. I am the receiving manager at a chemical manufacturing company. As soon as my insurance kicked in, I went back on anti-depressants. I take a different medication now and I saw a psychiatrist every other week for a year. He helped me to better understand how these medications affect my brain and how to spot signs they are no longer working. He taught me everyone's depression is different so I have to constantly watch out for those signs, and that medicine like that will always need to be adjusted and re-adjusted the longer I take them. I am pretty open with Declan about the medication and why I take it. I don't want to keep him in the dark about what depression is even though I pray that he never has to deal with it.

Getting off of the graveyard shift made a huge difference for me but truly everything about getting away from Sanson helped me. I wish I got out of there sooner. I get to eat dinner with my family every night AND I get weekends off! At Sanson when I didn't really talk to people, everyone thought I was an asshole. Here at Amresco I keep to myself and try not to talk to people that much and they just gave me an award for being "so focused" on my job! The differences are incredible.

A few days after I got out of the hospital I went to visit with Megan's Grandma Betty, she told me in a really sweet way that sooner or later everyone goes a little crazy. Everyone handles it differently but the important thing is to keep moving forward and not let it

drag you down. It was essentially the same thing my
dad, Megan and Barb all said to me but hearing it from
Betty made it stick with me. She had a way of saying
what you needed to hear in a non-judgmental way.
Her words told me to take care of myself but her eyes
told me to suck it up and take care of her grand-
daughter and her great-grandson. If I couldn't find a
good enough reason to live within myself then I had to
find my reasons to live in them. So that's what I do.

Even now, three years later I still have periods where
I feel like a failure but I can usually snap myself out
of it when I make Declan laugh or when Megan puts
her arms around me. I try really hard to stay positive
and focus on all that I do have instead of all that I
don't. Sometimes that means I can't watch the news
at night and sometimes it means that I can't be around
big gatherings. I have learned that all of that is OK.
The only way I can ever apologize for putting my
family through hell is to promise to get better every
day so that it never happens again.

The Hernia

I had a hernia when I was 19. I don't remember how it happened but I had a pretty severe pain in my nutsack and the next morning they were all swollen and I could hardly walk. Megan convinced me it wasn't normal and that I had to go to the doctor…in sweatpants!

My car at the time was a stick shift and Meg couldn't drive a stick shift so I had to as k Megan's grandma to drive because I couldn't change gears while holding my legs together. Do you know how embarrassing it is to have to ask your girlfriends grandma to drive you to the doctor because you are having severe nut trauma?

As the doctor was inspecting my junk he informed me that "the tear isn't that big, it can probably be fixed manually. Otherwise, you will need surgery..."

I asked what does manually mean? And he said all calmly "well, you have a tear at the top of your scrotum and your lower intestines are falling through. So I am gonna push your intestines back through that tear and hopefully enough scar tissue will develop to seal the rip naturally…But it's gonna hurt…"

Obviously, I was pretty stoked to have a 80 year-old man down there trying to poke a hole in one when he said, "Mr. MacKinnon, I know this is pretty uncomfortable but we have some medical students in the building today and this is something they don't get to see very often. Would you mind if they observed??"

How much worse could it be? So I said sure and Dr Thomas opened the door and yelled down the hall, "HEY KIDS, GET IN HERE. YOU GOTTA SEE THIS!!!!"

And in walks 4 of the hottest women I have ever seen in my life! It was like the goddamned Girls of the ER issue of Playboy magazine and I am laying on a (cold) exam table with no fucking pants on!!!

Because I am an idiot, I said to one medical student who was more embarrassed than I was, "So what brings you here this morning?" I was kind of proud I was able to make them laugh under such circumstances but then I remembered my dong was out and maybe I shouldn't make those playmates laugh...

Before I could regret my decision, Dr. Thomas was poking a very tender area. The pain was intense. I felt like I was gonna puke. I couldn't watch the doctor but the looks on the medical students faces told me that it must have been pretty brutal.

After 5 minutes or so, I actually heard a small pop and the pain lessened immediately. Dr. Thomas laughed and said, "GOT IT."

He gave me some painkillers and told me to ice my balls for a couple of days and to avoid strenuous activity. As the medical student left the room, I distinctly heard one girl say "wow", still not sure what she meant.

I put my sweatpants back on and grandma drove me back home. I never have had to have it surgically repaired so Dr. Thomas must have done a pretty good job, but I haven't trusted any doctors ever since...

The Stitches

When I was a kid, I was one of those kids whose tongue was always hanging out. Not in any kind of Michael Jordan impression or anything, just a kid with a big mouth and a Gene Simmons-sized tongue.

One fine summer day when I was about 11 or so, I played a game of pick up basketball at the Salvation Army. I took all 4ft, 4in of my body and tried to box out Mose s Malone for a rebound. An angry 7 footer's elbow came down on top of my head. The real problem was my tongue was sticking out at the time and I bit down. Hard. My teeth touched. It hurt, but not incredibly until I spit. And a GALLON of blood came out. All the guys on the other team yelled and were grossed out. I thought I must have bit my tongue pretty bad so I went to the bathroom to check it out. When I stuck my tongue out to see it, the whole thing almost fell out of my mouth!!! It was only hanging on by a little bit!

I got really scared and cried. I hopped on my bike and headed home. *Have you ever ridden your bike home while you crying but had to keep your mouth shut because every time you opened it giant pools of blood and drool fell out of your mouth? Not the best bike ride!* I threw down my bike and ran into the house. My mother was on the phone in the kitchen and I cried with my white T-shirt covered in blood, she had no reaction. "Listen, can I call you back? I have to take Lachlan to the hospital again."

I tried telling her what happened but it's hard to talk without a tongue...

She said, "Just get in the car". And we went to Rainbow where I had to get 20 stitches in my freaking tongue.

It was terrible. The same thing happened to me 2 more times before I figured out how to keep my tongue in my mouth.

Still working on how to keep my mouth shut...

ABOUT THE AUTHOR

Lachlan Mackinnon is a forklift operator and retired musician. He lives in Euclid, Ohio with his wife of 20 years and 11-year-old son. They have heard all of these stories before and are not amused. Let Me Tell You a Story is his first book.

98779990R00155

Made in the USA
Columbia, SC
05 July 2018